"Don't even think of it, Belinda!"

Vincent loomed over her, his eyes angrily mocking. "If you try to blackmail me, I'll make you sorry you ever set eyes on me!"

"I already am!" she snapped back.

He reached for her and she instinctively put her hands against his chest to shove him away. The contact was a physical shock and the instinct to fight him off suddenly died. Belinda couldn't think.

Only as he finally took her lips did she make a sound—a wild groan that forced itself out and was suffocated instantly by the hot pressure of his kiss. She must stop him. She hated this man—how could she let him touch her like this?

Belinda pulled away before he could say anything, and stumbled out of the room.

CHARLOTTE LAMB began to write "because it was one job I could do without having to leave the children." Now writing is her profession. She has had more than forty Harlequin novels published since 1978. "I love to write," she explains, "and it comes very easily to me." She and her family live in a beautiful old home on the Isle of Man, between England and Ireland. Charlotte spends eight hours a day writing—and enjoys every minute of it.

Books by Charlotte Lamb

HARLEQUIN PRESENTS

1001—HIDE AND SEEK
1025—CIRCLE OF FATE
1042—KISS OF FIRE
1059—WHIRLWIND
1081—ECHO OF PASSION
1106—OUT OF CONTROL
1170—NO MORE LONELY NIGHTS
1202—DESPERATION
1236—SEDUCTIVE STRANGER
1290—RUNAWAY WIFE
1345—RITES OF POSSESSION
1370—DARK PURSUIT

HARLEQUIN ROMANCE

2696—KINGFISHER MORNING
2804—THE HERON QUEST
2950—YOU CAN LOVE A STRANGER

CHARLOTTE LAMB

spellbinding

Harlequin Books

TORONTO • NEW YORK • LONDON
AMSTERDAM • PARIS • SYDNEY • HAMBURG
STOCKHOLM • ATHENS • TOKYO • MILAN

Harlequin Presents first edition September 1991
ISBN 0-373-11393-5

Original hardcover edition published in 1990
by Mills & Boon Limited

SPELLBINDING

CHAPTER ONE

BELINDA HUNT had been dead for months; dead, that was, to everything around her. Technically she was alive; her heart still beat, her lungs breathed in and out, but the only time she moved was when the nurses moved her, to guard against the dangerous side-effects of immobility. Belinda was unaware of that as she lay, like Snow White in a glass casket, her lids down over her green eyes, her head completely shaved at first, until the gold-streaked, coppery hair grew again, in silky little curls and then in full, rich waves which intensified the pallor of her face.

She was in the intensive care unit, a small but constantly busy department of a London hospital. The nurses who worked there kept up a lively chatter as they looked after her in the hope that one day their voices might penetrate the deathlike sleep which hung over her and stimulate a return to life.

'Doesn't it make you feel silly, talking to someone who doesn't even know you're there?' a new probationer asked Staff Nurse Hay one morning.

'We don't have a clue whether or not she can hear us!' said Hay, a neat and cheerful blonde woman in her twenties. 'But we have to keep trying. It's possible that constant stimulation works, so never forget to talk to her when you're doing anything for her.'

Nurse Lucas nodded hurriedly. 'Yes, Staff Nurse!' Small and mousy, she was eager to make a good impression; this was her first ward.

Staff Nurse Hay watched her thoughtfully, then relaxed and smiled, lowering her voice. 'Actually, Lucas, it helps us, too. We mustn't forget she's a human being, not just a doll we move around. Tell yourself she can hear you, she's just asleep, and it makes your job easier.' She bent down, her usual cheerful smile sounding in her voice. 'Hello, Belinda, how are you today? We're going to wash you, now, and comb your hair—visiting time in an hour! You want to look your best, don't you?'

'Do her family visit often?' the younger girl asked, helping to lift Belinda so that they could wash her.

Hay frowned and sighed. 'She hasn't really got a family. Her father died years ago, and her mother remarried. Lives in New Zealand now. She flew back after the accident, and came every day for a month, but she gave up hoping Belinda would come out of it. She couldn't stay anyway; she had other children, by the second husband, so she went home again.'

'But Belinda does get visitors?'

Hay smiled rather wryly. 'Oh, yes! One visitor's as regular as clockwork, and there are a few others.' Hay was washing Belinda's face as she talked, then began to brush her coppery hair slowly and gently.

Nurse Lucas, who was eighteen, with straight dark hair and dark eyes, watched in silence, thinking that Belinda was only a few years older than herself. 'How long has she been like this?' she asked Hay.

'Eight months.' Hay's voice was flat.

'Eight months? Oh. So, even if she did ever recover consciousness, she'd probably be brain-damaged?' Lucas burst out in shock.

Staff Nurse gave her a stern look. 'We don't know that!'

'But, probably——' began the young nurse, then stopped with a gasp, staring down at the patient.

'Lucas, never discuss a patient's prognosis in front of them, even if they're unconscious!' Staff Nurse Hay said sharply.

Nurse Lucas whispered, 'Staff! Staff... her eyelids moved!'

Staff Nurse Hay froze, staring at Belinda without seeing any change. She crossly said, 'Just automatic eye movement, Nurse——' She broke off, a shiver of primitive shock running down her back as the almost transparent blue-veined lids began to lift.

'I told you... I told you!' babbled Nurse Lucas excitedly.

They both gazed down at the slanted green eyes. Belinda wasn't yet focusing on anything; she was staring like a baby just beginning to see the world around it, myopically looking into a dazzle of light, blinking. Then the girl's pale lips parted and a breath came through them—a sound, almost like a sigh.

Staff Nurse Hay pulled herself together and, without taking her eyes from the patient, spoke softly and quickly to the probationer.

'Get Sister, she's in her office—ask her to get Mr Courteney, the specialist. Hurry, girl... don't just stand there dithering.'

Nurse Lucas reluctantly detached her eyes from Belinda and turned to run. The movement startled the girl in the bed; she suddenly seemed to realise that there were others in the room, and drew an audible breath, her pupils dilating as she looked around.

Staff Nurse Hay summoned up a soothing smile, bending down. 'Hello, Belinda. There's nothing to worry about. You're in hospital, you were involved in an accident, but you're going to be fine now, just fine.'

Belinda Hunt stared at the strange face, listening, feeling a troubling familiarity as if they had met in another world, although she couldn't remember it. She was bewildered, but she wasn't able to think about anything just now. The light was too bright. Everything in the room had a sharpness and clarity that hurt her eyes. Her lids slowly began to descend again, and Staff Nurse Hay urgently caught hold of her hand.

'Please...don't go back to sleep, Belinda. Stay awake. How do you feel? Anything I can get you?' Belinda licked her dry lips and the nurse at once said, 'Thirsty? Would you like some water?'

Belinda was barely aware of the question; she was frowning, trying to think. Where was she? What had happened? She moved her head slowly and looked at the woman in the white and blue uniform. Who was she?

As if reading the question from her face, the woman said gently, 'I'm Staff Nurse Hay. I've been looking after you since you came in; we're old friends, Belinda.'

So far the girl had not said a word; there was nothing in her pale, blank face to indicate that she understood what was being said to her, where she was, *anything*! Staff Nurse Hay's first exultant delight in seeing Belinda's eyes open began to dissolve into anxiety. Had irreparable brain damage been done? She had grown fond of her patient, and that was a mistake, she ruefully acknowledged to herself. It was unprofessional to get emotionally involved with a patient, that was one of the first lessons you learnt when you entered nursing, yet Hay could never help it. She liked people, that was why she had become a nurse in the first place, and, although she knew the score where a coma victim was concerned, she knew that some people did recover completely, and she had been hoping against hope that Belinda would be one of those who made it back to life without lasting consequence.

Belinda's lips parted again. Staff Nurse Hay leaned over to catch the faint, husky whisper.

'Ricky...' Belinda said. 'Where's Ricky?'

The nurse paled, frowning, and didn't answer. The door opened and Sister arrived with Mr Courteney and Nurse Lucas on her heels. The staff nurse drew back from the bed to greet the specialist, who gave her a nod. Sister Williams quietly reminded him of her name. She knew Mr Courteney had trouble remembering names, although he hated admitting as much.

'Staff Nurse Hay, sir.'

'I know that, Sister!' Mr Courteney said touchily. An elegant man with an austerely handsome face and silvered dark hair, the specialist had always been adored by the nurses who worked for him, and expected their hushed reverence. Before approaching the patient, he murmured very softly, 'Good morning, Staff Nurse Hay—this is excellent news! How long has she been conscious? Any idea what triggered it? What happened exactly?'

Hay answered as quietly, 'We were washing her, sir, when she opened her eyes.'

'Hmm... well, and how does she seem to you?' asked Mr Courteney, raising one fine silvered eyebrow. 'Has she said anything?'

Hay sighed. 'Just one thing, sir. She said, "Where's Ricky?"'

Mr Courteney drew in his lip. 'Ah. We may have a problem there. What did you tell her?'

'Nothing, sir. You arrived while I was wondering what to say.'

Mr Courteney grimaced. 'Very wise, Staff Nurse. We must all be discreet for the moment. Well, I'd better examine her.'

Sister Williams gave Hay a smile, nodding towards the door, and the staff nurse withdrew, taking Lucas with her. The probationer glanced back into the room before the door swung shut. She saw Belinda Hunt's face and was haunted by the lost, bewildered expression on it. What was she thinking about? How did it feel to be in Belinda's place—to wake up and discover you had been in a coma for months? And why had everyone looked so upset when Staff Nurse said that Belinda had asked about some guy called Ricky? Lucas was buzzing with questions, but she wasn't sure she ought to ask them. At the hospital they seemed to have a theory that probationers should be seen but not heard.

Belinda Hunt watched the door close. Why had that nurse given her such a strange look when she'd asked after Ricky? Coldness crept over her; she was suddenly afraid. She looked at the ward sister and the man in the white coat who was standing beside her now, smiling in a soothing fashion.

'Hello, Belinda! I'm looking after you while you're with us—my name is Courteney.'

'Hello, Doctor,' Belinda said in a faint, smoky voice, and he looked as delighted as if she had handed him a present. Everyone was reacting to her in such a strange way, she thought, puzzled. Had she been badly hurt in this accident? Funny that she couldn't remember anything about it. What exactly was wrong with her? A shudder of alarm went through her, but she didn't seem to be in pain or even to be bandaged in any way. She tentatively shifted her position and couldn't feel any discomfort. Her arms and legs seemed to be OK.

'I'm a specialist in neuro-surgery, Belinda. I operated on you when you first arrived.'

'N...n-euro-surgery...' Belinda stumbled over the word. 'I...I'm not sure what that means.'

Mr Courteney laughed as if she had made a very funny joke. 'I'm often not sure myself, Belinda—do you mind if I call you by your first name? I've known you so long now that I feel we're old friends.'

'I don't mind,' Belinda said slowly—hadn't that other nurse said something like that? She had said that they were 'old friends' by now. What did that imply? That she had been here in this hospital for quite a while? How long had she been here? Days? And what had happened to Ricky? Where was he? She had woken up thinking about Ricky, longing for him. Had he been hurt in this accident? She searched the surgeon's smiling face, wondering if he would tell her about Ricky. Or was the news so bad that they preferred to keep it from her? She had seen something in that nurse's face: a stricken look...pity, anxiety. Why should she have looked like that unless...unless something terrible had happened to Ricky in this accident?

'Did we crash?' she whispered. 'Ricky was driving, wasn't he?'

The surgeon and the ward sister didn't answer. They just watched her with the same expression she had seen in that other nurse's face; Belinda quivered with fear and pain. What weren't they telling her? He couldn't be dead...not Ricky, please God, not Ricky.

'I'd rather you didn't talk too much at first,' Mr Courteney said in a calm, smooth voice. 'We don't want to overtax your strength, do we? Now, I'm going to ask

you a few questions, and examine you, and then I'd like
you to have an X-ray.'

Belinda was afraid to ask any more questions then;
nor over the next couple of days while she underwent
what seemed to be an endless series of tests. The medical
team looking after her asked her enough questions,
heaven only knew; and so did a uniformed policeman
who came to see her. She could tell him nothing, since
she did not even remember the accident, and like
everyone else he seemed reluctant to answer any questions. For a while Belinda felt so weak that she hus-
banded her energy and saved her questions until she felt
more able to face the answers she suspected she might
get. If Ricky could come to see her, he would be here.
The fact that he did not come terrified her.

Whenever she was alone, except for the monitoring
nurse on duty behind a glass-panelled office in the centre
of the intensive-care unit, who saw and heard everything, she lay on her bed in the pastel-painted room,
thinking about Ricky, her mother, her job, her friends,
in a strange, remote way, as if she was remembering
something from long ago.

'We've been in touch with your mother,' she had been
told. 'She's flying over to see you at once. She'll be here
in three days' time.'

'You shouldn't have worried her!' Belinda had said.
'She can't afford to keep coming over here!'

Staff Nurse Hay had smiled. 'She'd never have forgiven us if we hadn't let her know! Last time, she came
the minute she heard about your accident, and stayed
for ages, but we had to tell her that you might not come
out of the coma for years, and there was no point in her
staying, so she went home. But she has rung up regularly

to find out how you are, and the minute she heard you
were conscious she couldn't wait to get on a plane!'

Belinda had been happy to hear that her mother was
coming. She hadn't seen her for several years. Her stepfather had always assured her that there was a home for
her in New Zealand, but, although she liked him and
was fond of her two little half-brothers, she had grown
up in London; it was her home and the place she felt
happiest. She missed her mother, but they wrote regularly; Belinda had always kept her mother in touch with
whatever she was doing—her job, her friends, the men
in her life, although they had never been very important
or special until she'd met Ricky. She had written pages
about Ricky, right from the first time they met.

'On a bus, Mum, would you believe? He saw me in
the park in my lunch hour. He was there, jogging, in a
tracksuit and trainers. He literally bumped into me on
the path, but I had to hurry back to work, so I had to
run, and he followed me on to my bus, came and sat
beside me and chatted me up...then realised he hadn't
got any money on him to pay his fare, so I paid, and
he took my address and said he'd pay me back, and all
the girls at work laughed at me and said I'd never see
him or my money again... But he came round to my
flat the same evening, with the money he owed me, and
a huge bouquet of flowers, and insisted on taking me
out to dinner at this fabulous restaurant, but I can't remember a thing I ate because I was too busy looking at
him and pinching myself because I couldn't believe he
was real. You should have seen the suit he was wearing!
Savile Row written all over it, Mum!'

She boasted to her mother about his elegant clothes,
but in fact Belinda secretly preferred him the way he had
looked in the park. Ricky was almost too good-looking,

that was the trouble—blond and blue-eyed, very slim, as lithe as a mountain cat in his black tracksuit, yet casual, approachable, on her own level. In his smoothly tailored suit he had seemed very different and it had bothered her.

He hadn't told her much about his background for weeks. She had picked up a few facts—that he worked in an office, had been to university but not done too well. 'I'm no great brain!' he'd grinned, and she had laughed and said neither was she, and so what? 'So what indeed?' he had said, kissing her. 'The way you look, who cares whether you have brains?'

'You took the words right out of my mouth!' she had teased, and he had roared with laughter. Ricky knew he was gorgeous, and he knew girls thought so, too. He had been frank with her about that, had admitted that there had been plenty of girls before she came into his life; it sometimes worried her, because how could she be sure he wouldn't tire of her the way he had of all the others? He said he loved her, she was the real thing at last—but had he ever said that before?

She soon discovered that he had a flat in Chelsea, where he lived alone. His family lived in Buckinghamshire. He vaguely mentioned his parents, both living, seemed fond of his mother and a little nervous of his father. She learnt that he had two brothers and a sister, all older than himself; that he had an old dog, a yellow Labrador, called Honey, of whom he was very fond and missed while he was in London, since his parents had her at their house in the country.

He not only ran and exercised daily, but he loved sport; he played tennis, rugby, cricket, squash . . . indeed, any competitive field sport. Ricky was very competitive. He liked to keep fit, and swam most days in the indoor pool in the basement of the block of flats where he lived. He was seven years older than Belinda—twenty-nine to her twenty-two. She felt that to be the perfect age gap, but then she thought everything about Ricky was perfect.

She was madly in love with him from about two minutes after they collided in that park on a fine autumn day, and to her joy Ricky seemed to feel the same way about her.

Staring at the window of her room, she saw a lilac tree in bud out in the hospital grounds; it was spring now. She had known Ricky for nine months and been happy almost every moment of that time, in spite of his family's opposition once they found out Ricky wanted to marry her.

His parents had been distantly polite in their hostility when Ricky had taken her home. It had been a big shock to her to discover what an enormous house they had; even more of a shock to realise how wealthy his family was, and she had had some doubts about the future as Ricky drove her home. His brothers and sister hadn't been present. Deirdre, his sister, was married and lived in Worcester with her two children, Belinda knew, and one of his brothers was also married, and lived in Ireland.

His mother had said something about what a pity it had been that Vincent was in America, and Ricky had gone red and changed the subject, leaving Belinda wondering if he had deliberately brought her to see his parents while his elder brother was away. She had known by then that Ricky was in awe of his brother, Vincent, and she had been curious to meet him.

Vincent Garrett actually ran the merchant bank for which Ricky worked. The family were major shareholders in the bank. Ricky hated his job; it was boring, he said frankly—but, having been such a flop at college, what else could he do? 'If only Vincent didn't run the place!' Ricky had groaned. 'He's a slave-driver. A terrifying guy, my big brother!'

Vincent must have found out about her visit to his home as soon as he got back from America, because two days later he arrived without warning at her home to catch her ready for bed in pink pyjamas and a shabby old woolly dressing-gown, having just had a bath and washed her hair, with bare feet, and wet hair hanging round her face.

Vincent Garrett had looked her up and down, his cold mouth twisting in derision. 'Miss Hunt? Belinda Hunt?' What had he been expecting? A *femme fatale* in a black satin backless nightdress? Judging by his face, he hadn't, anyway, anticipated being faced with a bedraggled creature dressed like a schoolgirl, and, staring at him, Belinda hadn't guessed who he was—why should she have done, when he looked nothing like Ricky? He was a very different type—that hard-boned, forbidding face, dark and brooding, with olive skin and light grey eyes, and a determined jawline.

'Yes,' she had admitted warily, clutching the door and barring his entry. Who on earth was he? He had stared icily into her puzzled eyes and told her, biting out the words through sharp, white teeth.

'I'm Vincent Garrett.'

'Ricky's brother?' she had gasped, appalled.

'Exactly,' he'd drawled. 'Do we have to talk on your doorstep?'

She had automatically fallen back and let him into her flat, apologising for the untidiness. It was only on the surface: a towel on a chair, where she had been rubbing her hair, a book on the floor, where she had been reading before he arrived, lounging on the carpet in front of the electric fire, a crumpled newspaper flung across the table.

It wouldn't have taken her two minutes to tidy up if she had known she was going to have a visitor, but as Vincent Garrett's icy eyes flicked around the small room she had flushed to her hairline, disliking him intensely. He had had as instant an effect on her as Ricky had done—but in reverse. She had loved Ricky almost on sight; she had hated Vincent, even before he gave her cause, before he told her why he had come.

She had begun by being polite, however. 'Would you like a drink?' It was second nature to her to be hospitable, even if he hadn't been an invited guest.

'No, thank you, nothing for me, I shall not be staying long,' he'd said crisply, standing in the centre of the room and facing her as if they were in aggressive confrontation. 'I'm going to be brutally frank, Miss Hunt. Ricky has told me all about you, and there's something I think you should know. Ricky should have told you, but he hasn't; he admitted as much to me. I know he's talked of marriage, but he can't marry you. He is going to marry a girl he has known for years. They got engaged two years ago——'

Belinda had made a choked sound of protest and disbelief, turning white, and the grey eyes had narrowed in scrutiny of her face.

'It's the truth,' Vincent Garrett had curtly insisted.

She had shaken her head, the curly tangles of wet hair against her neck. 'He'd have told me...'

'You don't know Ricky as well as you think you do,' he had said drily. 'Ricky always has preferred to ignore inconvenient facts. I've no doubt that when he first met you he didn't intend it to become a serious relationship, but, you see, Meg was determined to finish her university course and get a degree before she got married, so she made Ricky wait, and I think Ricky resented her insistence on that. She's had to spend the last year in France, teaching in a French school, so she and Ricky haven't been able to see each other—and Ricky's missed her and been lonely, which is why he picked you up. He still loves Meg, though. He always has. They've known each other since they were children; they're ideally suited.'

She had been stricken by the revelation about Ricky's life before they had met, by the discovery that he had once loved someone else, had got engaged, talked of marriage to another girl. Worse, he hadn't told her the truth.

He hadn't mentioned this girl, even when they had talked about old flames in a jokey way. 'None of my boyfriends made me laugh, and I must have a man with a sense of humour,' Belinda had said, smiling at him. 'What are your demands in a woman, Ricky?' and he had kissed her and said she met them all, she was just perfect. He had never hidden the fact that he'd dated lots of other girls in the past, but he hadn't mentioned anyone called Meg—what did she look like? Belinda had wondered jealously. Pretty? Had Ricky loved her? Or was Vincent Garrett lying?

'I don't believe you!' she had whispered huskily, shaking her head.

'You don't have to believe me,' Vincent had shrugged. 'Just ask Ricky.'

She had inwardly winced, already half believing, but hating him for having told her, and had broken out, 'You said you were going to be brutally frank, Mr Garrett, so tell me this—the truth is that your family don't think I'm good enough for Ricky. I'm just an ordinary working girl, I don't come from your world, and you don't want me marrying your brother, do you?'

She had forced down her misery and fear, and faced him in challenge, her green eyes spitting angry resentment. Vincent Garret had stared coolly at her, a glint of curiosity in his eyes, but otherwise impervious to anything she could throw at him, a hard-bitten, remote man armoured in his wealth and assurance.

'No, I don't want you marrying my brother,' he had admitted with a dry smile.

'And this other girl... the one you claim he is engaged to... she is suitable, I suppose?' Belinda had said bitterly. 'Which means she has a family background, money—all the things I don't have?'

'Meg's family does have money,' he grated, 'but that has nothing to do with it.'

'Oh, of course not!' Belinda had laughed without amusement. 'It sounds to me as if you and your family have picked out a wife for Ricky, and he refuses to be a good little boy. He actually wants to pick his own wife! It must be infuriating for you.'

'Nothing of the kind!' Vincent Garrett had snapped, and she had eyed him scornfully.

'No? Well, if any of that farrago of nonsense you just told me is true, Ricky himself can tell me. I'm certain Ricky loves me—I know he does—and he wouldn't lie to me, but I don't trust you, so please go away.'

She had marched to the door and flung it open and he had advanced towards her, frowning blackly, but he hadn't left, he had grabbed her by the shoulders and shaken her like a rag doll, his long fingers hurting her. 'Have you been sleeping with him? Is that why you're so sure he loves you?' he had demanded hoarsely.

She had pulled free, dark red and trembling with rage. 'Mind your own business!'

'I'm making this my business! I want to know how far this has gone—so tell me! Have you slept with him?' His voice had been harsh, his face a threat, inches away from hers, and she had obstinately refused to tell him the truth.

'What if I have? It has nothing to do with you!'

He had almost hurled her away from him, and the next instant he had gone, and she had stood there trembling violently as if she had been exposed to a hurricane, a tempest, some elemental thing which destroyed and rushed on leaving everything wrecked in its path. Vincent Garrett had a darkness in him, a core of violence which terrified her, leaving her unable to move for what seemed a very long time.

She had rung Ricky half an hour later, when she had dressed in jeans and a sweater, tied her hair back from her face in a pony-tail, put on some make-up, made herself feel more normal and able to talk without losing control or bursting into tears.

Ricky had been expecting her call, that much was obvious. 'I'm sorry, I tried to tell you over and over again,' he said miserably. 'Darling, I couldn't ... I was afraid of losing you if you knew about her, but you see it's over, her and me, finished ages ago, once I'd met you. I love you, darling; say you forgive me for keeping it from you. I want to marry you, not Meg ...'

She had forgiven him; she loved him too much to do anything else. That weekend they had driven down to his family home to face the whole family: parents, brothers, sister.

Ricky had said he had told them how he felt, and that he was going to marry Belinda, not Meg, and they accepted it, but Belinda had still been shaky with nerves as they drove through summer sunshine.

'What about your brother?' she had asked anxiously, and Ricky had pulled a face.

'Oh, Vincent will come round...' He hadn't sounded too sure, and Belinda hadn't been very optimistic either. She hated Vincent Garrett and she feared him, in more or less equal proportions, and she did not have much hope that he would soften towards her. He didn't want her marrying his brother, and his opposition would be formidable. She had not been looking forward to seeing him again.

That was the last thing she remembered—that drive through the countryside. She lay there thinking about it, realising what must have happened—she didn't remember an accident. One minute she had been in the car with Ricky, feeling edgy and dry-mouthed, and the next she'd been swallowed up into a great black void to emerge here, in this room, knowing nothing of what had intervened. How long had she been here? How had the accident happened? What had happened to Ricky? She didn't know, but when she felt strong enough, maybe when her mother was here to back her up, she was going to make the hospital staff give her a few answers.

The door of her room opened and she turned her head reluctantly, expecting to see Staff Nurse Hay with her latest medication, or Mr Courteney with another of his little examinations in mind.

It was neither of them. It was a tall, black-haired man in a navy-blue cashmere overcoat. Across the small room their eyes met: his hard, grey, searching her face with an intense scrutiny; hers wide and shocked and appalled.

She remembered him only too well from their one and only meeting. How could she ever forget—or forgive— Vincent Garrett?

CHAPTER TWO

'YOU!' Belinda muttered, her hands gripping the sheet in a jerky movement, as if she meant to yank it up to her face and hide behind it, which, in fact, she was tempted to do, except that she wouldn't give him the satisfaction of seeing her betray her fear of him. 'What are you doing here?'

He came into the room and quietly closed the door, then walked towards her bed, still staring at her, making her very aware of the way the delicate, lace-trimmed white nightdress she was wearing revealed her bare shoulders and the deep valley between her breasts. She had only just begun to wear her own clothes again after months of wearing white cotton hospital gowns. Staff Nurse had produced this nightdress, saying that her mother had bought it for her not long after the accident and, since her mother was expected that evening and might visit her as soon as she arrived, she had decided to put on the nightdress, but now she wished she hadn't. She didn't like the way Vincent Garrett's cool eyes flicked over her body and back up to her face.

'I was beginning to think you'd never open your eyes again,' that deep, dark voice said, and the familiarity of it was a shock to her, somehow. She hadn't expected to remember him so sharply.

She frowned—had he been in this room before? Seen her unconscious, unaware of his presence? She hated the thought of that; it made her edgy to imagine Vincent

Garrett standing beside her watching her while she was so totally oblivious of him.

He was carrying something which he had held out of her line of vision until now when he lifted it and laid it on her bedside table. 'You've woken up just in time for spring!'

She stared at the huge bouquet of spring flowers: golden daffodils, white narcissis, pink tulips, blue irises. Her face burned in the surprise of it, but of course he had brought her flowers out of courtesy—people always brought you flowers when you were in hospital, didn't they? It was an automatic gesture. She answered it with equally automatic politeness.

'Thank you, they're lovely.' She didn't feel like being polite to him, but it had been kind of him to visit her. Why had he come, though? He had scarcely known her; he certainly had not liked her. So why was he here? She suddenly remembered Ricky's bringing her flowers, the day they had first met. Her eyes glazed with unshed tears and her throat hurt when she tried to swallow. She knew, didn't she? She knew why Ricky's brother had come to visit her. Beware the Greeks when they come bearing gifts, wasn't that what people said? Well, no doubt he felt guilty about his hostility to her now.

Belinda bit down on her inner lip, tasting the salt of blood, and fought to get control of herself. She didn't look at Vincent, but she knew he was watching her with remote, hard eyes. His smooth cashmere coat hung open over one of those formal city suits he and Ricky always seemed to wear for work; just as they wore red or blue striped tailored shirts, with stiff collars, and quietly elegant silk ties. She had hated to see Ricky in them. They made him seem alien to her. Vincent Garrett would always be alien to her, whatever he wore. He was armoured in his wealth and arrogance. He shrugged out of the coat and laid it over a chair, pulled up another chair and sat down, crossing one leg over the other casually, as if he meant to stay for some time.

She waited for him to say something, to tell her what he had come here to say, but there was a silence, so she took a deep breath, took her courage in both hands and said bravely, 'Tell me.'

He just went on staring at her as if he didn't know what she meant, but he knew, of course he knew. With a mixture of anger and fear she said, 'Tell me about Ricky.'

There was a silence, and she watched him, her mouth quivering, her skin ashen. Vincent's eyes probed her face—she could guess he was trying to decide whether or not she was strong enough to hear the news—and she fixedly gazed back, words exploding from her like lava from a volcano.

'I've got to know. Tell me. I've been asking about him ever since I woke up, but nobody will say anything, and it's driving me crazy. He's dead, isn't he? He was killed in the crash, that's why they won't tell me, they're afraid the shock will be bad for me, but the suspense is worse, believe me! I can stand it, whatever it is; please tell me!'

Vincent considered her coolly, his grey eyes narrowed on her as if she were a specimen under a microscope, then shrugged his broad shoulders. 'Well, you have to know sooner or later, I suppose. I promised your specialist I wouldn't tell you yet, but I think you're right—guessing and not being told is probably worse than the truth. Ricky isn't dead——'

'Oh...' Belinda shook with such urgent relief that it was like a stab of pain. She closed her eyes, sighing deeply, and for a moment Vincent Garrett didn't go on, he just sat in silence watching her, until she opened her eyes again and gave him a searching look as her relief gave way to fresh anxiety.

'But he was hurt? Badly? Is he in the hospital here?'

'No, he wasn't hurt—at least, not badly. A few cuts and grazes, a couple of broken ribs, nothing much. He was lucky.' Vincent's hard mouth twisted coldly. 'Ricky always is.'

'Then why hasn't he been to see me since I recovered consciousness?' Belinda said slowly, frowning. 'Why have the hospital staff been so uneasy whenever I mentioned him? There's something wrong, I know there is!' She tried to sit up and Vincent Garrett immediately rose to push her back against her pillow, his powerful hands closing on her bare arms and sending an electric shudder of rejection through her. 'Don't touch me!' she groaned out on impulse. 'Don't ever touch me!'

He straightened, and Belinda felt afraid suddenly. His eyes were icy with menace, his face frigid. He hadn't liked her reaction to him, but so what? He had always been her enemy; why should she hide her dislike? Especially now when she knew that her worst fears were groundless. Ricky was alive—so why hadn't he been to see her? She could guess; she should have known.

'You're keeping Ricky away from me,' she accused. 'That's it, isn't it? You've forbidden him to come and see me! You've told the hospital staff to keep him out.'

'Oh, for——' He broke off a furious swear word, grimacing. 'I realise you enjoy blaming me, I'm a useful scapegoat, but no! I have not forbidden Ricky to do anything, nor have I given orders to the hospital to keep him out.'

'Then why hasn't he been——?' she began, and he interrupted tersely.

'Ricky is married.'

For a split second she couldn't believe what he had said; her green eyes widened and darkened, the pupils glittering like jet, her skin totally without colour and her mouth trembling.

'No! It's a lie, I don't believe you,' she whispered. 'It can't be true, Ricky wouldn't... We were getting married, he loved me...'

Vincent Garrett's voice was wintrily expressionless, and so was his face—that dark, impenetrable face she had always feared. 'He was married a week ago. They're in the Caribbean on honeymoon, a very long honeymoon. They're sailing Meg's father's yacht around the islands. They won't be back for several months.'

Belinda shook her head silently, her mouth parched, her lips framing the word, 'No.' It couldn't be true, she thought wildly; Ricky wouldn't marry that other girl, he loved her, he wouldn't betray her like this. She wanted to cry out in anguish, to deny it, to refuse to believe, but she knew he was telling the truth. There would be no point in lying, after all; she could so easily find out if it was true—and it explained so much: the looks of pity she had been getting whenever she mentioned Ricky to the medical staff, their embarrassed silences and hurried changes of subject.

She looked at Vincent with bitter hostility. 'So you got your own way, after all! But you always meant to, somehow. Lucky for you that we crashed, wasn't it? You must have been over the moon when you heard that I was in a coma. It gave you the chance you'd been looking for.'

He didn't reply, his face a stern mask, and Belinda burned with a hatred which almost shocked her with its intensity. 'I know you scared him,' she ground out, her green eyes violent with pain. 'Ricky told me you were ruthless, but he was underestimating you, wasn't he? With me safely out of the way you had Ricky backed into a corner, and I'm sure you used every weapon you could think of to get him to marry that girl.'

He was so cool, so icily sure of himself, sitting there staring at her without emotion, quite indifferent to the pain he had inflicted on her. He didn't care a damn what he had done to her. He only cared about his own plans, his own wishes. He had no emotions, of course. The man was incapable of them.

'I shouldn't have broken it to you so abruptly,' he muttered, almost to himself, frowning. 'That doctor was right; you weren't ready to hear the news. I realise it helps to put all the blame on me, and I'm not going to lie and say I didn't want Ricky to marry Meg, but, believe me, I am sorry you had to get hurt like this——'

'Get out of here!' she snapped, her hands tightening into fists on the bed. How dared he sympathise with her, look at her that way? She didn't want him feeling sorry for her; the very idea made her throat sting with bile. After what he had done to wreck her life, how dared he? 'Get out before I hit you. I'm tempted to, I swear I'm tempted to...' She was distraught, shaking, tears in her eyes. 'I'd like to hit you so hard that I draw blood. I hope one day someone hurts you the way you've deliberately hurt me, that's all, and I'd love to be around to see it!' At least that seemed to have made him frown, his mouth a white line, and his skin drawn tightly over his strong bones, but his grey eyes stayed as hard as flint, because nothing she could say could touch him. She began to shake with the desire to hit out violently. 'Get out of my sight! I hate you!' she cried out hoarsely, then picked up his flowers and threw them at him. 'And take these with you! I want nothing from you. Nothing at all.'

The flowers fell to the floor and spilled everywhere in bright, sweet-smelling disorder. Vincent Garrett got up, stepping over the golden trumpets of daffodils, the dark, velvety blue of irises, looming over her bed, a very tall, very powerful figure, and dangerous, in spite of the civilised formality of his clothes. While she was screaming at him she had seen the barbaric force of the man under those expensive clothes; they were a thin disguise for an insistent will for power and domination.

'You're hysterical,' was all he said. 'I'll get a nurse.' She hadn't made any impression on that adamantine nature. You would need a sledgehammer to break through the iron surface and reach the man inside.

'Just get out, and never come near me again!' she threw after him as he strode to the door.

He vanished and a moment later Staff Nurse Hay came quickly into the room, her face anxious. Belinda was lying on her side by then, her face buried in the pillow, the tears raining down her cheeks.

'You poor kid!' Hay said, hurrying over to the bed, and Belinda rubbed a hand angrily over her wet face, keeping her head averted.

'Leave me alone. Please.' The last thing she needed was an audience; her pride was smarting enough already, especially since she realised that Hay must know that Ricky had jilted her and married someone else. They all knew; they were all sorry for her, and she hated their pity.

The mumbled plea was met by a sigh, but Hay didn't go, she just said in a quiet voice, 'I will, in a minute, but first I'm going to give you something to calm you down and help you sleep, OK?'

Belinda didn't argue; she was glad to escape from the misery of her thoughts into sleep. At that precise moment, she almost wished she had never come out of the coma. At least while she was unconscious all those months she had not known that Ricky had deserted her.

Did he ever really love me? she kept wondering. Had he meant a word he said? How could he have, if he was ready to marry someone else in such a short time?

Her mother arrived late that evening, her face pale, her eyes red-rimmed from lack of sleep and the weariness of jet lag. Tears welled up as she ran towards the bed, arms outstretched. 'Bell! Oh, Bell, darling. I prayed for a miracle and it has happened.'

Why didn't it happen before Ricky married someone else? Belinda thought bitterly, but she pushed the thought aside, hugging her mother. 'It's lovely to see you. Thanks for coming all this way!'

'I only wish we could all have come. We couldn't afford it, though, darling. Jack and the boys send their love; we were so thrilled when we heard. I've brought cards and presents from everyone, and all the love in the world. I promised them I'd give you a kiss from each of them, so here goes! This is from Jack, this is from Billy, and this is from Steve.'

Belinda accepted the three kisses, moved. Her mother's second family might be on the other side of the world, but she still felt very close to them all. 'I wish they could have come, too!' she told Rosemary Clifford, and her mother sat down on a chair beside her bed, clutching a carrier bag stuffed full of wrapped parcels, which she poured out on to the bedcover.

'Shall I open them now?' asked Belinda, hoping her sadness didn't show because she didn't want to worry her mother. It wasn't easy to look cheerful; her smile felt stiff and phoney, but she made herself go on beaming like a lighthouse.

'Of course! Then I can tell Jack and the boys how you liked their prezzies,' said Rosemary Clifford, watching her daughter opening each parcel, exclaiming over the contents: a nightie from her stepfather, Jack; a book from the elder boy, Billy, perfumed soaps from little Steve. Belinda read each card aloud, touched by the loving messages and feeling less lonely, less betrayed. Ricky had walked out on her, but she still had her family. She had been feeling so alone, but now her mother was here, and she felt better.

Mrs Clifford didn't stay long that day; she was too exhausted after her long flight from New Zealand. She staggered off after half an hour, promising to be back next afternoon, but in fact did not appear again until the evening visiting hour when she paid Belinda another brief visit.

'I'm sorry, I couldn't get here this afternoon—I slept all day. I'm suffering from jet lag,' she moaned, a hand to her temples. 'Oh, my head! If you knew…the agony… I've never had a headache like it! I'm sorry, darling, I won't be able to stay long tonight, either. I must get some more sleep. I feel dreadful! I've never made that flight without a stop-over en route, at Singapore or Hong Kong, and I never will again, let me tell you!'

Belinda smiled wearily. 'Don't worry about it, Mother. I'm quite tired, too. They keep me sedated most of the time. If you stayed I wouldn't be good company.'

Mrs Clifford was much brighter the following afternoon. She stayed for well over an hour, promising to come back later that day, but before she arrived that evening Belinda had another visitor, a friend from her office, Tracy Beamish, a small, quiet girl, like a neat squirrel, with dark brown eyes and tiny hands and feet who scampered rather than ran everywhere, and had a permanent expression of wary alertness. She brought cards and flowers from the other people who worked for their firm, a large insurance brokers with offices all over Great Britain.

'Everyone's so kind,' Belinda said, staring at the massed ranks of cards now lined up on the window-sill and on every flat surface around the hospital room. There were flowers everywhere, too; the room was a garden, the air full of a heady scent of spring. She should feel loved and cherished. She wished she did, instead of this chill, aching misery which seemed to possess every part of her. As it was, her only other option was to pretend, and she did, like mad, smiling too brightly, laughing too loudly, hoping Tracy didn't notice the artificiality of her cheerful manner.

'What will you do when you leave here?' asked Tracy before she left, and Belinda was taken aback by the question. It hadn't occurred to her before that one day she would leave the hospital.

'Well, it won't be for some time, apparently,' she said slowly, frowning.

'No, of course not, but what I meant was...when you've completely recovered, are you coming back to the office? I'm sure the firm will be glad to take you back. Of course, this new girl is doing your actual job, but there are plenty of other jobs you could do.'

Belinda swallowed, realising that Tracy, too, knew that Ricky had jilted her and married someone else. The girls in the office had given her an engagement present only a short time before the crash. It was humiliating to guess at the gossip that had gone on since her accident. She didn't think she could face them all.

'I haven't thought about it yet. It might be an idea to try something new.'

Tracy's brown eyes held bright interest. 'Yes, I suppose that after what happened—I mean, the coma, being unconscious all those months—it must seem odd, coming back to life. All sorts of things have happened while you were...' she paused, choosing her word carefully, a little flush on her face '...away, so to speak...and you don't know about them. People will have changed. I mean, old Mr Danvers who'd been with the firm for twenty years, he died the other day, on his way home from work. And Annie Derby got married last month...and——' She broke off, biting her lip and looking embarrassed.

'Yes, exactly,' said Belinda, hiding the flinch she couldn't help at this reminder of Ricky's wedding. 'Life moved on, but I didn't, and maybe it would be better if I looked around for a new job when I'm well enough.'

'Oh, Bell, I'm sorry...' burst out Tracy, then, embarrassed, hurried off home, on the verge of tears, leaving Belinda staring at the wall with fixed attention. It had become one of her ways of controlling her grief; she stared at nothing until her mind was calmer and the threat of tears had diminished. By the time her mother arrived, she was able to greet her with one of the cheerful smiles she had learnt to give even when she was in the depths of misery.

Mrs Clifford stayed on in London for several weeks, and would have stayed longer if Belinda had not insisted that she must get back to her other children. 'Wonderful though it is to have you here, I know the boys need you more than I do now that I'm getting better every day.'

'Thank God!' agreed her mother fervently, and Belinda nodded, smiling.

'I'm going to be fine now, Mum,' she assured Mrs Clifford. 'You don't have to worry about me.'

'I will, though,' her mother said uneasily, giving her a sideways look which Belinda grimly recognised. They had not discussed Ricky yet. Belinda had steered clear of the subject, and Rosemary Clifford had taken her lead and discreetly never mentioned him. 'You've had a bad time,' began her mother, and she said harshly,

'Don't talk about it, Mother!'

There was a silence. Mrs Clifford sighed audibly. 'If that's what you want... Bell, darling, when you can leave the hospital, why don't you come home?' She laughed. 'I mean, come out to us, to New Zealand? You know I'd love it, and Jack and the boys want you to come; they'd be so thrilled to have you back with us. I talked to them all about it, and they told me to say it would be just wonderful if you'd come. Will you?'

Belinda hesitated, torn between the comforting idea of becoming part of a family again, protected and cosseted, and the knowledge that she still felt most at home in London, and was, anyway, used to being an adult, in charge of her own life, making her own decisions, and even her own mistakes.

'Maybe later, Mum,' she said at last. 'I'd love to come, but not yet. First, let me get used to looking after myself again.'

She missed her mother during the weeks that followed, but she was working hard with a physiotherapist to restore her wasted muscles, and her days were busy enough to stop her feeling lonely, although she did have problems on her mind. She was beginning to realise exactly what her missing eight months had cost her. Not only had she lost Ricky; she had in effect lost her job, even if the company were prepared to offer her another one, and she had lost her home. Her landlord brought her a bunch of flowers and unhappily admitted he had relet her flat when her lease ran out. 'I couldn't afford to keep your flat empty forever,' he apologised. 'And . . . well, nobody seemed sure if . . . when you would recover.'

So her flat had been let to another tenant and her possessions had been packed up and stored for her.

It was that which showed Belinda that nobody had really expected her to recover from her coma. It wasn't just Ricky who had abandoned her. The whole world had given up on her. It was a deep shock to her. It made her feel she had come back from the dead.

'You'll be OK, though,' Hay comforted while she was massaging Belinda's legs one morning. 'I expect your mother has got lawyers working on the insurance claim, hasn't she? That should be a lot of money!'

That hadn't occurred to Belinda. She stared, guessing that it hadn't occurred to her mother, either. Her mother hadn't mentioned any claim for compensation—and surely she would have done if any case had been in hand?

'And when you leave here, you'll be going to a convalescent home for a month or so,' said Hay. 'Plenty of time to find yourself a new home when you're completely back to normal.'

That was the first Belinda had heard of a convalescent home. 'How soon do I go?' she asked and Hay grinned at her.

'Eager to leave us? That's nice, after all we've done for you! No, I'm just teasing. I'm glad you're feeling so well. It will be a while yet, before you're ready to leave. The physiotherapist doesn't think you're ready yet, even though you're beginning to walk quite well.'

'Where is this convalescent home?'

'I'm not sure which one they'll send you to, but it will be in the country, somewhere pretty—they always are. You stay there for a month under observation, but having a holiday at the same time. After such a long illness, you see, you need time to adjust to being out of hospital before you have to plunge back into everyday life.'

'And to do that I'll need a new home and a new job!' Belinda bleakly pointed out.

'Now, stop worrying,' said Hay. 'There's plenty of time to start fretting over problems when you're quite better. You'll get help over all that. You don't need to worry about a thing.'

Belinda wasn't listening; she was thinking hard, her green eyes fierce. 'I want to see a solicitor,' she said. 'I don't believe my mother has consulted one about my accident, and you're right—I must be entitled to compensation. How do I go about getting hold of a lawyer?'

Hay looked startled. 'I don't know, that isn't my province. Can't it wait, though? You shouldn't be bothering your head with lawyers at the moment.'

'The sooner I put in a claim, the better, surely?'

'Oh, well, maybe. I'll ask the hospital almoner to pop down to see you some time—it is her job to deal with things like that.'

Belinda was satisfied with that and relaxed, but it wasn't the hospital almoner who came to see her that afternoon. It was Vincent Garrett.

She was lying on top of her bed, wearing green silk pyjamas and a matching kimono-style dressing-gown, her mother's parting gift, listening to the hospital radio on headphones while she read a magazine. When the door opened she didn't hear or notice until she suddenly sensed a movement and turned her head, her green eyes wide and startled.

The shock of recognition hit her like a speeding truck. She dropped her magazine and started to get off the bed, only to be pulled back by the headphones.

'Careful!' Vincent moved swiftly to help her unravel herself and their hands touched.

The contact was brief, but electric. Belinda shot back, off the bed, facing him across it, her breathing much too rapid, a flush of heat in her cheeks.

'I told you never to come near me again!' She wanted to sound icy and was furious with herself to hear a note of panic in her voice. That was what she felt at the sight of him; but she didn't want him to know that.

He observed her, his black brows together, a strange fixity of attention in his grey eyes.

'You look——' he began, and broke off, his mouth twisting in an irony she didn't understand, even though she read it clearly. 'Much better,' he finished coolly, but that was not what he had been going to say.

'Go away!' she muttered, backing towards the window.

'I shouldn't stand there,' he drawled, taking off his cashmere overcoat.

'I'll stand where I like!' She leaned against the window-sill, her stance defiant, her chin lifted, a slender, shimmering figure in the delicate silk kimono, her vibrant hair haloed by the sun. She wasn't taking orders from him, or even advice. She wanted nothing from him, nothing at all, and she wished he wouldn't stare like that. What was he thinking? Something in his face disturbed her.

'Just as you choose, of course, but I just wondered if you knew that with the light behind you that delightful outfit becomes almost transparent,' he said, mockery in his eyes.

That didn't help her panic much. She leapt away from the window, her flush deepened to a burning red, hating him.

'How dare you come here?' she burst out, her voice shaking. 'Haven't you done enough to me already? You and your brother have wrecked my life. I've got no home, no job, I've lost eight months of my life and...and...Ricky...' She stopped, swallowing a bitterness that made speech impossible for a moment.

'If you're wise, you'll forget you ever met Ricky!' he grated, his brows forbidding.

'Oh, I'm sure you'd like that!' she muttered.

She hated the man watching her, this man with remote eyes like cold steel and a hard-boned, arrogant face. He had been her enemy from the start; one look and he had despised her, been icily determined that she should not be allowed to marry his brother, and he had won, hadn't he? What he wanted had come to pass, and she had lost everything. She looked at him and wanted to kill him, but there was another way she could hit back at Vincent Garrett, and she meant to take it.

The only thing he really cared about was money, and that was where she could hurt him—by making him give her a fortune in exchange for everything he had taken from her.

'I shall be seeing a lawyer tomorrow,' she said in a level voice, hoping to sound as cool as he usually did. 'I'm going to sue your brother. It is going to cost him a fortune to compensate me for all the damage that accident did to me.'

CHAPTER THREE

VINCENT GARRETT pulled a chair away from the wall and coolly sat down, crossing his long legs and flicking open the jacket of his elegantly styled dark suit. Belinda couldn't help watching; the way he moved was hypnotically watchable, but he knew it and that annoyed her. She wouldn't give him the satisfaction of imagining that she found him attractive. She didn't. She hated him far too much. It was just that the man had class; he carried the glitter of utter confidence and style, and no woman could help being fascinated by that. Such assurance always made you look twice.

'So!' he drawled. 'It was his money you wanted, after all!' and that made her turn white and then crimson.

She looked at him savagely. 'I might have known you'd counter attack by making vicious remarks like that. Well, I won't even bother to answer! I'm not descending to your level. Your brother wrecked my life, and any court will award me damages. That's all I have to say to you, so please leave, will you?' Belinda wished she could stay calm, but her voice shook and she had difficulty controlling her face. Hatred was as engrossing and as exhausting as love, she was discovering. She loathed this man, yet she couldn't take her eyes off him and every movement he made registered on her own body in electric flashes of awareness.

He made no attempt to get up again, nor did he show any signs of meaning to leave. Instead, he raised one brow sardonically and enquired in a dry tone, 'How much do you imagine you'll get?'

She glared. 'My lawyer will deal with all that.'

'Oh, come on, you might give me an idea how greedy you're going to be so that I can warn my brother as soon as he gets back. Or were you hoping I'd ruin his honeymoon by getting in touch to tell him what you were threatening?'

She climbed back into her bed, pulled the covers over her shoulders, and turned her back on him, deciding that the only way to cope with his insults was to ignore him altogether.

He waited a moment, then said, 'If you want to blame somebody, blame me——'

'I do!'

He laughed curtly. 'I realise you feel bitter.'

'How understanding of you!'

He gave an impatient sigh. 'If you're wise, you'll forget Ricky. Don't try to destroy his marriage; that won't make you feel any happier.'

'I'm talking about making an insurance claim, I'm not threatening to destroy his marriage!'

'The crash was an accident. It wasn't Ricky's fault— you're being unfair if you blame him.' He paused, then added quietly, 'And it was months before he abandoned hope that you would get better, you know.'

She turned then, angrily flushing. 'And every time he looked around you made sure *she* was there, oozing sympathy! I'm sure you rushed her back from France as soon as you heard about the crash. It was your big chance, wasn't it? And you didn't waste a second grabbing it.'

'You're hysterical,' he said, and of course he was right, she was, but how could she help it? 'Meg came back as soon as she heard Ricky had had an accident, but I didn't suggest she came. I didn't need to—as far as Meg knew, she had every right to rush to his side. They were still engaged. Ricky hadn't told her he'd changed his mind.'

That was a shock. Belinda lay still, frozen, her green eyes wide and stunned. 'That's a lie,' she whispered when she could speak, but she knew it was true. She had believed Ricky had told Meg it was all over between them, but she knew Ricky hated facing up to things. He would have put off telling Meg. He would have wanted to wait, to find the right moment, which had never arrived.

'Perhaps he hadn't quite made up his mind,' said Vincent, and she reacted to that violently.

'That's what you want to think, isn't it? You can't bear to believe he might have loved me! Well, he convinced me he did, he swore he loved me, but all he did was ruin my life. When I get out of here I shall have to start again, with a new job, a new home, and your brother is going to have to pay for what he did to me.'

'Well, if money is all it takes to heal your broken heart...' drawled Vincent insultingly.

She drew a fierce breath, so furious that she couldn't get a word out. He left before she managed it, his footsteps very loud in the quiet room. She heard the sound with a sense of intense familiarity, as though she had often heard him leave like that before.

Had he ever come while she'd been in a coma? she wondered with a start. It wasn't the first time she had had such odd thoughts. She often felt she was almost remembering sounds she had heard during those long months asleep: a voice, a footstep, a movement. It couldn't be so, of course, yet still the sense of *déjà vu* persisted.

Why had Vincent Garrett come today—today of all days? He had stayed away for weeks, ever since she'd screamed at him to get out and stay away from her. She had thought she would never see him again, and that suited her. Yet here he was again—why? Or why now?

Had he kept in touch with the hospital, and discovered that she was so much better that she would soon be allowed to leave and go to a convalescent home? Had he come today to find out her plans for the future? Vincent Garrett was a shrewd man. A cynical man. He must have been waiting to hear from her lawyers for months; he could probably guess exactly how much compensation she would be able to claim.

She laughed bitterly, her eyes savage. Maybe he had been hoping she would die and solve the problem?

Well, now he could warn his lawyers to expect trouble, and she must find herself a lawyer, too. It would take years to fight the case, anyway; she was aware of that. The law was a slow process. The sooner you started the wheels rolling, the better.

She didn't feel up to talking to anyone else today, though. She would deal with it tomorrow. It was a distasteful prospect; the idea of it making her sick. She closed her eyes and felt intolerably lonely. Ricky was in a yacht on a sunlit sea with his new wife; he hadn't suffered any lasting consequences of the crash. She was the only one who had been badly hurt—in every sense of the word.

She had every right to demand compensation, hadn't she? If Ricky had been a total stranger, nobody would be surprised to hear that she was suing him. Accident victims did it every day. Why should she feel guilty? Why should she let Vincent Garrett make her feel guilty?

She suddenly remembered talking to Hay about seeing a solicitor—surely Hay hadn't told Vincent Garrett about their conversation? No, she wouldn't have done that!

Belinda stared at nothing, frowning. Am I getting paranoid? Hay? I don't believe she would conspire against me. It was an odd coincidence, though, that he should turn up so soon afterwards, wasn't it?

Hay came into the room a few minutes later and Belinda looked into her friendly eyes uneasily, wishing she did not feel this awful suspicion. Hay was so nice. How could she suspect her? But Vincent Garrett was an attractive man—a powerful one, too. Belinda hated the man, but she had picked up the distinct impression that all the nurses rather fancied him.

'Did you ever ask the almoner to come and see me, Hay?' she quietly asked, and Hay smiled, nodding.

'Yes, she said she would deal with it. Has she been yet?'

'Not yet,' Belinda said, wondering if it had been the hospital authorities who had let Vincent Garrett know she was planning to consult a solicitor. She preferred to believe that. She liked Hay.

'I'll jog her memory!' Hay said cheerfully, tidying the room in her usual deft, efficient way.

'No, give her another day or so; she's probably busy,' said Belinda, who was curious to see if the almoner would actually come at all.

She didn't. To Belinda that seemed to prove the case against this unknown woman. She must have rung Vincent. No doubt he had asked her to keep him informed of Belinda's progress. He had probably said that, as Ricky's brother, he felt responsible for her; he must have claimed some sort of right to know how she was! Why else should the almoner have told him she was talking of seeing a solicitor? And no doubt he had promptly told the almoner he would deal with the situation, she need not go and see Belinda, she could leave it all to him! Oh, yes! That was his style. The bland arrogance, the smiling determination to get his own way.

Belinda had plenty of time to think about him. She lay awake at night a lot lately; she had spent so much time asleep, she supposed, that it was quite natural for her to have a touch of insomnia, and thinking about the iniquities of Vincent Garrett helped her through the long night.

It was several weeks before she was considered strong enough to leave the hospital for a month in a convalescent home. She was excited by the thought of going out into the outside world, even though she felt at the same time a *frisson* of nerves at the prospect.

'We'll miss you,' Hay said, almost tearful, when Belinda gave her the red and black raw silk scarf she had got Tracy to buy for her, along with little gifts for the other nurses she had grown to know so well.

'Thanks for everything you've done; I know how much I owe you,' Belinda said shyly to them all, but they brushed her thanks aside.

'It was a pleasure,' Hay said for them all. 'That's our job. We enjoy looking after people, in fact, that's why we do it, and it's great to see someone making such a wonderful recovery after being so ill. You've made us all feel ten feet tall by getting better, believe me.'

'I hope the nurses at this convalescent home are as nice,' said Belinda, smiling. 'I only wish you were all coming with me!'

'Oh, the atmosphere will be quite different there. More like a hotel than a hospital. You won't be needing nursing now.' Hay looked at the watch pinned to her apron bib. 'The car should be here soon. Have you got everything? I'll come down to wave you off!'

Belinda made it into the lift and downstairs on her own two feet, and was so proud of this achievement that she was flushing and laughing as she said goodbye to Hay while the hospital porter put her luggage into the waiting car.

'Send us a postcard, let us know how you are!' reminded Hay as they hugged each other.

'Of course I will!' Belinda said huskily.

Hay had become a friend over these long, painful weeks of recovery. Belinda owed her more than she could ever repay, but she liked her, too. The hospital had become her home and she was afraid of leaving it. Tears spilled down her face; she turned and dived into the car to hide her emotion, but turned her head to wave back at Hay as the car began to move away smoothly, down the long drive towards the hospital gates.

Only as the little group on the steps of the hospital vanished from her sight did she turn her eyes on to the man in the driving seat, and then her body jerked in icy shock.

'What the...what's going on?' she broke out, her voice hoarse with breathless incredulity and jagged alarm. She hardly believed her eyes. What was he doing behind the wheel of the car?

'Do up your seatbelt,' was all Vincent Garrett said without even looking at her, and that didn't help to alleviate her fears.

She didn't obey him; she said in a voice she tried without success to keep very level, 'Stop this car at once and let me out!' If she sounded confident enough, he might take her seriously.

'Do up your seatbelt,' he repeated in that cold, auth-
oritative voice. She could only see part of his face, in
the driving mirror: his dark hair, the winged line of his
brows, those remote, pale grey eyes. He was as cool as
an ice-cube.

'Are you kidnapping me?' Belinda challenged angrily.

In the mirror his eyes narrowed on her face briefly,
before returning to their scrutiny of the road. 'Nothing
so melodramatic. I'm merely driving you to the convalescent home. Now, do up your seatbelt, will you?'
His voice stung like a whip.

She automatically did up the belt, frowning. Being in
a car again reminded her of the last time. 'How did the
accident happen?' she wondered aloud.

He threw her another sharp, searching glance in the
mirror. 'You mean nobody told you the details? Another
car went out of control and spun straight into the path
of Ricky's car. He braked as hard as he could, and the
crash would have been a damn sight worse if Ricky
hadn't been so quick-thinking.'

Her mouth twisted. 'Well? Go on. Finish it.'

'Finish what?'

'The point you're making.'

'And what's that?'

'That I shouldn't blame Ricky for what happened, and
I must give up any idea of claiming compensation. That's
what you're really saying, isn't it?'

'I was just telling you what nobody had apparently
told you before—the true facts of the accident.'

'How you see them, you mean. We'll let a court decide
how true your version is, shall we? I'm not ready to
accept your word for anything.' She turned and looked
sideways out of the car at the grey London suburban
streets through which they were now driving. She knew

London quite well, but she did not recognise any land-
marks, until she suddenly caught sight of a roadsign.
They were heading north, it seemed.

'Why are you driving me?' she thought aloud. 'You're
a busy man; a very important man, as you went to great
pains to make me realise the first time we met. You made
it clear that I was a nobody, not fit to clean your shoes.
So why are you wasting your very valuable time driving
me about? And where are you taking me, anyway?'

'Didn't they tell you?' he answered smoothly, picking
up speed as he entered a northbound motorway junction.
'A private nursing home called Dillingham Place. Very
comfortable, delightful gardens and a friendly atmosphere. You'll enjoy your stay there.'

'Where is it?' she asked with suspicion. He hadn't
answered her first question. Why was he driving her?
Why him, not a hospital driver? Or even a taxi driver?

'Buckinghamshire,' he said calmly, and her whole
body stiffened.

'Buckinghamshire? But that's where...'

'Where my family live,' he agreed. 'Yes.'

She stared at his reflected face in the little mirror. It
didn't reveal anything of what might be in his mind.
'How far from their house is this nursing home?' she
demanded.

'Approximately?' he drawled in that infuriatingly
bland tone, and the back of her neck prickled.

'Exactly how far?'

'Exactly?' He pretended to consider, his head to one
side. 'Oh, half a mile, I suppose.'

Her mind whirled with questions, but it was a little
while before she could manage to ask any of them. 'Why
am I going to a nursing home which is so close to where
your family live? Don't try to kid me that it's a coinci-

dence, because I won't buy it. You're up to something— what is it?'

He answered smoothly—far too smoothly. 'Dillingham Place is a private nursing home run by a company which happens to be a client of my bank.'

'Oh, it just happens to be one of your clients, does it?' she bit out. 'Well, I can't afford the cost of private treatment!'

'You won't have to pay.'

'Who will be paying, then?' She bit her lip, her eyes wide and glazed with unshed tears. 'Ricky? It's Ricky, isn't it? He's going to pay for me to have this month in a private home? Well, I'm not taking a penny from him!' She had forgotten for a moment her sworn resolve to make Ricky pay for what he had done to her. 'He isn't buying his way out of trouble,' she muttered. 'He needn't think he is! Take me back to London, I'm not booking into this nursing home!'

'Ricky isn't paying!' Vincent said when she stopped, her voice shaking and husky. She looked at him scornfully.

'It has to be him; don't try and lie to me. Who else could it be?'

'I am paying,' he said, and she stopped dead, really taken aback now.

'You?' She couldn't think straight for a moment; Vincent had taken her completely by surprise, but then her mind began to work again and she realised what it all meant. Did they really think she was so stupid that she wouldn't see through their little plot?

'Of course,' she said with sarcasm. 'It would be you who would pay. That way Ricky wouldn't be accepting or admitting any responsibility for my condition. Clever. Which of you thought that one up?'

'Ricky isn't involved at all. He doesn't even know you have come out of the coma yet,' Vincent said quietly, and a jab of pain went through her.

Ricky was on his honeymoon; he had forgotten all about her. She fell silent, fighting with the misery of knowing that the man she had loved so much was in the arms of another woman. She had been so sure she had found a real love, one that would last forever. But it had died without her even knowing; she had slept while Ricky left her.

She wished she could hate Ricky the way she hated his brother, but love, or the memory of it, clung like poison ivy; it stung like it, too. Her mother had always said she was obstinate. 'Stubborn as an ox, Bell—aren't you?' she would sigh. 'You won't change your mind or budge an inch. One day you'll hurt yourself.' Well, she was hurting herself now. She should start forgetting Ricky the way he had forgotten her; she knew that, but she didn't know how. Her heart was as obstinate as her mind. She leaned back in silence, staring out of the car.

They were travelling through green countryside now, with an occasional village, and glimpses of black and white cows grazing in meadows whose hedges were white with May flowers, the honey-scented, starry blossoms of the hawthorn. Bluebells made a hazy blue smoke under the trees in a little wood. Spring was halfway to summer. She had missed several seasons, slept through them, like a hibernating animal, and the realisation made her look at everything with a greater clarity of vision, with a more poignant sense of how lovely it all was, and how fleeting.

The car slowed. 'We're here,' Vincent said.

Belinda sat up, focusing on the open gates through which he swung the car. Ahead she saw a long drive between beech trees; their smooth, silvery bark glistening in sunlight. Yellow catkins clustered among the light, green leaves, shaken by a spring wind to drift down the air as golden dust which clung to the windscreen of the car.

The house was a gracious Edwardian building with a red-tiled roof and white walls. Belinda looked for signs of other patients, or hospital staff, but there was only a gardener, in green cord trousers and boots, pushing a wheelbarrow along a path round the side of the house.

Vincent pulled up, got out, and strode round to open her door and help her out of the car.

Belinda would have refused to leave the car, but she was exhausted by the journey. She did not have the energy to argue. Her legs had gone to sleep during the long drive; she stumbled as she took her first step, and clutched at Vincent instinctively. He put an arm around her, staring into her pale face, then picked her up into his arms and carried her towards the house.

'Put me down!' she broke out, as flushed now as she had been pale.

'You're not up to walking!' Vincent said drily, and tightened his hold. She was disturbed by being held in his arms, her head against his chest, his heart beating right under her ear. That close physical contact was having a strange and worrying effect on her. Hatred had odd side-effects; she felt her own heartbeat shaking her body as if she had thunder caged inside her.

The front door swung open as they approached it, and a woman in a dark green pleated wool dress smiled at them both cheerfully. 'There you are, Vincent! I was just wondering if you would be here in time for tea when I heard your car in the drive, so I put the kettle on!'

She must know him well to use his first name, Belinda recognised—was she the owner of this nursing home?

And the bank's client? She was small and slight, silver-haired, yet with such a lively face that it was quite impossible to guess her age.

Belinda managed a polite little smile in answer to the all-over inspection of the blue eyes.

'Was the journey too much for you, my dear? Would you like to go straight to bed? Vincent, take her upstairs——'

'No, I'm fine,' Belinda hurriedly said, seeing an open door across the panelled hall and the leap of firelight on polished wood. Presumably the other patients would be in there, having their tea, and she would rather meet them than have Vincent carry her up to her bedroom. The situation was intimate enough already. 'I'm dying for a cup of tea.'

'Very well, a quick cup of tea, and then bed,' said Vincent in that high-handed way.

She bristled. 'And I can walk! Please put me down.'

Vincent ignored that, striding across the hall and into an elegant room furnished in the Edwardian style of the house, with pink and white striped chintz sofas, matching curtains, and art nouveau furniture, including an octagonal tea-table covered with an embroidered tablecloth, which was laid with a very pretty rose-sprigged bone-china tea service.

Belinda looked eagerly around for the other patients, but the room was empty. 'Where is everyone?' she asked as Vincent gently deposited her on a sofa and tucked a cushion behind her head.

The older woman looked bewildered. 'Everyone?'

'The others,' said Belinda, frowning.

Vincent intervened. 'I haven't introduced you yet, have I? Jess, this is Belinda Hunt, of course. Belinda, this is Jess Mintern, who's in charge of us all, and terrifies the life out of me, so be careful to do as she says, won't you?'

The elegant woman eyed him sideways. 'Don't talk nonsense, Vincent! Take no notice, Belinda; if I can do anything for you, just ask. That's what I'm here for, that's what Vincent really meant—I run the house, and I hope you're going to be very happy here.'

She held out a thin, work-worn hand and Belinda took it, smiling. She liked this woman with the gentle eyes and the soft voice, and Jess smiled back at her as if she felt the same immediate impulse of friendship.

'I'm sure I shall like it; it seems a very pleasant place,' Belinda said politely.

'And there's plenty to do,' Vincent said. 'There's an indoor pool, horses in the stables, a billiard table—and, if all else fails, you can take healthy walks in the fresh air. You get great views from the hill up there...' He pointed towards the window through which she could see a green hillside looming above the house.

'Oh, I'm sure Belinda isn't going to be bored,' Jess Mintern said drily, an odd expression on her face. 'Now, if you'll both excuse me, I'll go and make that tea.' She hurried out and Vincent stood on the hearth, his face coolly blank, but there was something behind his grey eyes—a watchful alertness that made Belinda frown. She was beginning to get to know him, to catch expressions in his face that warned her he was hiding something, even conspiring against her at times.

'Where are the other patients? Aren't they going to join us for tea?' she asked him, and he shrugged, his broad shoulders indifferent, not answering.

'Are they out? Or in their rooms?' she persisted and he regarded her in the same waiting silence. Belinda felt another leap of alarm. He was definitely keeping something from her, and she began, rather incredulously, to suspect what that was.

'There are other patients, aren't there?' she asked, turning paler.

Vincent just watched her, his face cool and blank.

'Are there any? Tell me the truth!' she demanded.

'No,' he murmured, and for a moment she couldn't believe her ears, even though the fact had been slowly dawning on her. She gabbled to give herself time to think what this meant, what was happening to her.

'What do you mean, no? I can't be the only one.'

'The only one,' he agreed nonchalantly, a strange glint in his grey eyes, and he even dared to smile, a mocking little smile that sent furious blood rushing to her head.

'There are no other patients at all? Just me? What on earth is going on? This isn't a convalescent home, and that woman isn't a nurse. Who is she?' Her green eyes widened as the full implications began to burst on her. 'Or should I ask, what is she? Have I been kidnapped, after all, and is she my gaoler?' She swung her legs down from the sofa and stood up, angry to find she was shaking. 'I'm not staying here, I'm leaving.' She glared at him as she found her way to the door barred by his long, lean body. 'Don't you dare try to stop me!' she hoarsely threatened him.

'Don't be stupid, Belinda,' he said curtly. All the amusement and mockery had gone from his face; it had hardened and there was a glitter of impatience in his eyes, but he took an audible breath and tried to speak gently. 'Sit down again—you've been very ill for months, and you're in no condition to go charging around like this!'

'I'm leaving!' She stepped sideways to go round him, but he merely shifted position to bar her way again, so she pushed him angrily, her hands flat on his chest. 'Get out of my way!'

For a brief time this afternoon, she had begun to glimpse a Vincent Garrett who could have charm, even warmth; but the other man was back, the cold, remote, hard man who had deliberately set out to destroy her relationship with Ricky.

'You aren't going anywhere!' he said, gripping her wrists and trying to push her backwards on to the sofa.

She struggled, her face white and bitter with resentment. 'Don't you dare touch me! I can't stand having you anywhere near me!'

Something flashed in his face, a white-hot rage, a fury that made him look even more dangerous and sent a jab of fear through Belinda. She suddenly felt it might, after all, be wise to obey him and sit down, but she was too late. Before she could move, Vincent's grip on her wrists tightened like iron handcuffs. She was wrenched forward at speed until her body hit his. The impact made her breathless, her lips parting in a weak gasp of shock.

Vincent's mouth came down like the sword of an avenging angel and she shuddered at the force and power unleashed against her. For a second she simply stood there, shaking, unable to think clearly. It wasn't happening—it couldn't be happening. Vincent Garrett hated her. Almost as much as she hated him. The very thought of his kissing her made her want to throw up. Her eyes stayed wide open, her face was white, then red. It is a punishment, she thought; he can't hit me so he is kissing me, inflicting himself on me.

Vincent let go of her wrists suddenly; his arms went round her and held her tightly, so close that she couldn't breathe and began to feel she might faint. This is hatred, she thought; there is no faking the violence of this emotion. She felt it raging in him as his mouth crushed down, and an answering fury rose in her. She shook with it, growing dizzy, and had to close her eyes and hang on to Vincent to stay on her feet, her body limp in his arms.

The rattle of a tea-trolley approaching broke them both out of it. Vincent lifted his head, his lips reluctantly leaving hers. Belinda could hardly breathe; she opened her eyes, her skin so heated that she felt feverish, and risked a brief, hurried look at him. He was staring down at her and he looked dazed, as if the violence that had been unleashed inside him had been almost as shattering to him as it had to her.

He had released her now. Belinda backed, trembling, and sank backwards on to the sofa as the door opened.

'Teatime!' Jess Mintern said cheerfully as she came into the room, pushing her trolley.

CHAPTER FOUR

JESS did not appear aware of the atmosphere, which to Belinda seemed so heavy with emotion. She just picked up the delicate Georgian silver teapot, gave Belinda a smile and asked, 'How do you like your tea? Strong or weak? Milk? Sugar?' Belinda mumbled some sort of answer in a husky voice, wondering how Jess could be so blind to the tension in the air. When she risked a swift, secret glance at Vincent through her lowered lashes she incredulously found him looking as cool and collected as if nothing had ever happened, too. Belinda's brain reeled. She hadn't imagined that kiss. Had she?

'Give Belinda her tea, Vincent,' said Jess, and he took the cup and brought it over, handing it to her with a polite smile.

'I hope that's how you like it,' he said, and Belinda wanted to scream, half believing some hidden innuendo in the apparently courteous question, but she didn't scream, of course. She had to pretend that everything was normal. If they could hide behind bland masks, so could she, so she swallowed her mounting rage and somehow forced a smile.

'Yes, thank you. That's perfect.' The tea was straw-coloured, scented. China tea, she thought, inhaling the fragrance, staring into the liquid as if it fascinated her. She wished she had gone to bed now, but she had to sit this out; she wasn't running away. That might give Vincent the idea that she was scared of him, and she must not do that. She had to make him think he didn't

bother her in the least. That was one thing she had learnt
long ago, when she was a child, at school—if you faced
up to bullies they usually ran away themselves; if you
showed fear, they had won. Surely Vincent would go
soon? She didn't look up, but she was aware of him
accepting a cup of tea, and she bit down into her lower
lip. Oh, why didn't he go? His presence grated on her
and she was really feeling weary now. She was dying to
lie down, to sleep.

'You have no family in England now, I gather?' Jess
Mintern asked, and Belinda looked up, nodding, a
wistful look in her eyes for a second before she hid it
by looking away.

'Well, no close relatives, anyway. My father is dead,
and my mother has remarried. She lives in New Zealand
now.' She didn't look at Vincent Garrett, but she was
aiming her next words at him, her voice smokily hostile.
'I've promised to join them there when I'm well enough
for the long flight. I must ring them tomorrow to let
them know where I am. Is there a pay-phone here?' She
looked enquiringly at Jess, who gave her a sympathetic
smile.

'You can use the phone whenever you like, dear.
There's one in your room.'

'Oh, thank you. I won't make long-distance calls all
the time, don't worry, but I would like to ring New
Zealand just this once. They knew I was moving to a
convalescent home, but I didn't let them know the address. I suppose they can always get it from the hospital
authorities, but I would like to talk to my mother for
five minutes.' She wanted Vincent to know she had a
family who would be concerned about her. He needn't
think she was alone in the world, and defenceless. She

gave him a swift, wary look and found him watching her, his face cold.

'They already know,' he said tersely, and she did a double-take then, her face pale and disbelieving.

'They know? What do you mean? How could they...? I mean, what makes you think that? Did the hospital let them know, is that what you mean?'

'I did. I told your mother on the telephone, before making the arrangements. I felt I should ask her permission to go ahead, and she was happy to give it.'

Belinda was stunned. Her mother knew all about Ricky, the pain he had caused her, the bitter legacy of their broken love-affair, and the part the Garrett family, and, above all, Vincent Garrett, had played in his betrayal. Her mother must surely have realised how she would hate being here as Vincent's guest, eating food he had paid for, having to put up with his company—even if she couldn't guess that it would mean being in some strange fashion in his power, for that was how it felt, as though Vincent had brought her here a prisoner and meant to keep her one, too.

Belinda pushed back the rich coppery waves of hair which had fallen over her face. She didn't believe him; her mother wouldn't have agreed. Unless Vincent had lied to her. What had he really told her mother?

'Some Madeira cake?' asked Jess Mintern kindly, a slice of the cake proffered on a plate, but Belinda shook her head, swallowing.

'No, thank you. I...I really think I'd like to go to bed now.' She shrank back in her chair, afraid that he would try to carry her up the stairs the way he had carried her into this house, but at that instant the telephone rang, and Jess turned her head to listen, then looked at Vincent with a wry little smile.

'That will be Magdalen.'

Vincent froze in his tracks. 'What?' His voice was sharp, his features taut. Belinda stiffened, watching him alertly.

Jess was watching him, too, her expression unreadable to Belinda. 'Yes, she has rung three times this afternoon already. I told her you would be back around teatime.'

'You didn't tell her——?' Vincent broke off the question, giving Belinda a strange sidelong glance. Belinda stared back, startled to see a faint redness in his face.

'No, I didn't,' Jess said drily, clearly understanding whatever he had not said.

'Thanks, Jess.' Vincent gave her a rueful smile.

'You'd better answer that before it stops ringing!' Jess merely said, shaking her head at him as if in reprimand.

Vincent loped towards the door, then vanished into the hallway. After a few seconds, the phone stopped ringing. Belinda vaguely picked up the sound of his deep voice talking somewhere; she heard his laughing, and herself began to frown. Who was Magdalen? His latest woman? Was it serious, or just a passing affair? Not that it mattered to her, of course! She was just curious. And what hadn't he wanted Jess to tell this other woman?

About me? she wondered. Was that it? Had Vincent been afraid that Jess might have let it drop that he was driving Belinda down from London? If Magdalen meant more to him than just a light romance, she might know his family—and might have heard all about Belinda. Maybe Vincent was afraid his girlfriend would get the wrong idea? Maybe she was the jealous sort?

Belinda's green eyes flashed. Magdalen need not fret, there was no danger of her stealing Vincent Garrett—in fact, she wouldn't have him on a silver platter with an apple in his mouth! Although the image was certainly an intriguing one, she thought with bleak humour.

Of course, it might be simpler than that. Vincent might not have told his family that he was bringing Belinda to Dillingham Place; he might not want them to know of her presence so close to their own home, and might be afraid that Magdalen would tell them if she found out.

Yes, that made more sense. He wouldn't want his family to know he was still seeing the girl who had almost ruined their plans for Ricky. They probably hoped she would never show up in their lives again. They must think she was a problem solved, all her nuisance-value dealt with by Ricky's marriage.

Her face hardened, her pallor intensifying. Well, they were wrong. She meant to be a thorn in their flesh for a long time to come. They had ruined her life, and she meant to return the compliment, even if she had to use their weapons to do it. Money was all they understood— so she would use money to hurt them. Vincent need not think that by paying for her convalescence here he was going to soften her heart and make her change her mind about suing his brother. Somehow or other, she was going to make them all pay for what they had done to her, especially Vincent himself.

'Well, if you'd like to go to your room now...' Jess said, breaking in on her brooding thoughts, and Belinda pulled herself together to smile.

'Oh, yes, thank you.'

Jess moved to help her up, but Belinda shook her head. 'I can manage, honestly!'

Jess stood back, smiling, but followed her to the door, staying close enough to help if Belinda faltered. They met Vincent in the hall, striding towards them.

'I have to go,' he said, his cool eyes flicking over Belinda in a way she did not like.

'Goodbye, Mr Garrett,' she said icily.

'I'll be seeing you,' he drily returned, and to Belinda that sounded like a threat. The last thing she wanted was to see Vincent Garrett again.

'If you need me, Jess, you know where to find me,' he said as he left, then the front door slammed and Belinda wearily climbed the stairs with Jess right behind her, as though afraid she might suddenly tumble back down again.

'This is your room,' Jess said, flinging open a door on the wide landing.

Belinda was too tired to look at the room; she concentrated on taking a last few steps, and hardly noticed anything before she made it to a pink velvet chair and sank down with a long sigh. Jess was there at once, concern in her face. 'Are you OK?' She picked up Belinda's wrist and took her pulse, watching her pale face closely. 'Any headache? Dizziness?'

'No, nothing like that. I'll live,' Belinda said with a wry smile as she got her breath back. 'The stairs were just too much for me, I suppose.'

'Well, let's get you into bed now. I won't be keeping you there, don't worry. From tomorrow you can suit yourself, but just for today I think you'd be better off in bed, don't you?'

Belinda wasn't arguing. She got undressed and into bed, and Jess closed the curtains, plunging the room into blueish shadow. Outside in the garden Belinda heard birds calling in the dusk, and in the house a comfortable silence reigned.

'There's a jug of water on the bedside table, and a glass,' said Jess. 'Do you think you'll be able to eat dinner?'

Belinda shook her head, her lids heavy. 'I'm sorry, would you mind if I skip it tonight? I'd just like to go to sleep.'

'I think you're very wise. The drive from London was probably exhausting, especially as it was the first time you've been in a car since your accident. If you need me, there's a bell push right next to you—do you see it?' Jess pointed and Belinda looked obediently at the red button, nodding. Her eyelids were as heavy as lead now. She longed for Jess to go.

Jess went to the door and looked back. 'Goodnight, then. Sure there's nothing else I can do for you?'

Belinda let her lids droop; through them she saw the room in a haze and Jess seemed very far away. Sleepily Belinda opened her mouth, meaning to just say goodnight. Instead, since Jess was so distant and the question was on her mind, she asked, 'Are you really a nurse?'

'Fully qualified,' said Jess, watching her with a faint frown. 'I worked in a hospital for years—why, are you in pain? Don't keep it to yourself if something's wrong—tell me!'

'Nothing's wrong, I just wondered . . . is this a nursing home?'

'A nursing home? Of course it isn't.' Jess came back, anxiety in her voice, and put a hand on Belinda's forehead. 'Are you feverish? No, temperature's low, if anything. It must be because you're so tired that you're babbling. Go to sleep now, there's a good girl.' She smoothed a hand down over Belinda's eyes. 'Go to sleep.'

Belinda did, consumed by sleep as if it were some giant wave crashing down over her and swallowing her up.

When she woke up the room was full of pale sunlight, and she was quite recovered, all her weariness gone. She lay in the bed looking around with alert eyes which took in everything. It was a spacious room, furnished delightfully. The bed was ultra comfortable, she had slept like an angel under a goose-feather duvet which was inside a gorgeous pink and cream Liberty print cover. The whole room echoed that design; this was an Edwardian room, yet with modern comforts. She loved the rose-pink art nouveau curtains, the cream deep-piled carpet, the art nouveau wallpaper which carried the same design as the curtains, the exquisitely framed mirror of the same period, the Celtic-style carving on the dressing-table legs, and on the wardrobe and chest which matched it.

Belinda was enchanted, and lay there for ages, staring. After the starch and starkness of the hospital, this room was in another world. She hadn't been expecting anything so beautiful. Surely all nursing homes weren't like this? she thought, then it hit her—the memory of her brief exchange with Jess last night, in the moments before sleep had engulfed her.

This was not a nursing home! Jess had said so, hadn't she? Of course it wasn't a nursing home, she had said, looking at Belinda as if her brain might have given way!

Belinda went cold with shock at the memory. But if this wasn't a nursing home, why had Vincent Garrett brought her here? What was this place? Who was Jess? Another memory came back to her. Jess was at least a qualified nurse. That was something. Or was it? If this was not a nursing home, why was a qualified nurse acting as her hostess?

What was happening to her? Fear made her mouth dry, and, realising how thirsty she was, she reached for the jug of water beside her, only to knock a small clock off the bedside table.

The resulting crash made her jump and sit upright, horrified. She leaned over to pick up the clock. Please, please don't be broken! she thought as she looked down at it, and was relieved to hear it ticking, and to see no visible signs of damage.

A moment later the door swung open and she flinched, looking across the room at Jess.

'Are you all right? I heard a bang.' The older woman hurried towards her, and Belinda shakily confessed to the accident.

'I don't think the clock is broken, though.'

Jess took it from her and replaced it on the table, smiling at her. 'Don't worry about it. How do you feel this morning? You look better, but I'd better take your temperature and pulse before I let you get up, just to make sure.'

Both were fine, and Jess allowed her to get up and take a bath before getting dressed in a simple white blouse and pleated grey skirt, her small waist encircled by a narrow black leather belt. Belinda stared at herself in the mirror as she brushed her long, coppery hair and tied it back at the nape with a white ribbon bow. Her face betrayed her uncertainty and alarm; she fought to look calm. She must seem relaxed; she had to make Jess think she was just fine. She wanted to make friends with Jess. She instinctively liked her, and she couldn't believe Jess would be involved in anything dangerous or illegal, so either Vincent had not told her the truth about whatever he was up to, or Belinda was imagining things and there was nothing sinister going on at all.

'Were you always this tiny, or have you lost a lot of weight since your accident?' asked Jess with a grin as Belinda joined her downstairs.

'I was always slim, but not this skinny!' Belinda said, grimacing. 'Apparently they had me on a drip while I was unconscious, but I still lost a lot of weight. I'm not sure what they were putting into me...'

'Saline and glucose, I expect. It helps to keep you alive.' Jess smiled at her as she showed the way into a sunlit room filled with the delicious smell of coffee. 'But scrambled eggs and mushrooms taste better.'

That was what Belinda had for breakfast and she found she had a surprising appetite. The food was brought in by a young woman in a white apron who nodded cheerfully to her. 'This is Lucy,' Jess said. 'She's in charge of the kitchen. I don't cook, I'm afraid. Years of working in hospitals left me hopeless in a kitchen.'

'Hello, Lucy,' Belinda politely said.

'Hello.' Lucy was short and sturdily built with a determined chin and brown hair. There was a glint of curiosity in her brown eyes, but she merely said, 'If you have any special likes or dislikes where food's concerned, let me know, won't you? I hope you enjoy your breakfast.'

When she had gone, Jess excused herself too. 'I'll leave you to eat in peace, then maybe you would like to look around the house, or as it's such a nice day you might sit outside in the sun for half an hour? If you want me later, I'll be upstairs unpacking your case and doing your room.'

'Oh, I can unpack; please don't feel you have to do everything for me! I must start looking after myself again.'

'It's no trouble to me—you don't seem to have much luggage. You still have to take things easy for a while, you know. Now, eat your breakfast before it gets cold.'

When Jess had gone, Belinda obediently ate. The food was good, and so was the coffee served with it. Afterwards, she stood by the open window for a while, staring out into the garden, breathing in the sweet scent of roses, feeling the sunlight warming her cheek, and filled with contentment.

I'm alive, and I could be dead, she thought, the idea hitting her with real force for the first time. In the hospital her days had been quiet and faintly depressing. This morning, though, she actually felt alive; more, she was aware of feeling happy.

She wandered out of the dining-room to look for Jess and heard the sound of a vacuum cleaner in one of the rooms along the hall. She glanced in at the door of a sitting-room, but the room was empty, and she was about to turn away again when Ricky's face leapt towards her. She froze on the spot, staring at the silver photograph frame which stood on top of a piano, then slowly crossed the room to pick it up. His eyes held a smile she remembered only too well—she had fallen headlong for that boyish charm and the faintly rakish good looks and smooth blond hair. Tears filled her eyes. She had almost forgotten what he looked like, and now the memory was sharp and painful.

She brushed the back of her hand across her eyes, dropping the photograph with a clatter which made her jump.

Her nerves were in a bad way. She picked up the silver photograph frame again and carefully set it back in its place, then a thought struck her with blinding force.

What on earth was a photo of Ricky doing here? She looked quickly at the other photographs arranged in a little cluster on the piano, her eyes widening. They were all of the Garrett family!

There were Ricky's parents, laughing happily, his father's arm around his mother; another was of Ricky again, with Vincent, and the yellow Labrador dog, Honey, who lived with the Garrett parents although she was really Ricky's dog. The photo must have been taken years ago—both the men looked far younger than they did today, but not as young as they looked in a family group which included their sister, Deirdre, in a wedding dress and veil, smiling radiantly beside her new husband.

Belinda's eyes slowly moved on to the next photo: Vincent again, this time with a very beautiful girl with smooth black hair and dark eyes. Was she a member of the Garrett clan? Belinda had never seen her before, but it was certainly a striking photograph. The two of them were casually dressed: Vincent wasn't wearing a tie, his shirt was open, his skin had a suntanned look, and the girl was in a summer dress. They looked relaxed, at ease together; the girl's arm was through Vincent's, and she was leaning on him, a sensual smile on her full mouth.

Lovers, thought Belinda, with a strange sinking sensation in her stomach. They were lovers, these two.

She looked again at the girl's smile, and felt sick. She looked at Vincent's arrogantly self-confident features, and hatred burned in her throat. Someone ought to teach that man a lesson, wreck his love-affair the way he had carefully wrecked hers.

Did he plan to marry this girl? She was lovely enough, and she had the right air of self-assurance. Her dress seemed expensive, she was well-groomed, glamorous, sleekly sophisticated. No doubt she came from a suitable family—she looked as if she had always had money. She would be welcomed by the Garretts with open arms.

Belinda picked up the photograph; her angry eyes travelled over the faces again, and then she noticed the writing on the bottom of the picture. At first she couldn't read the message; she had to peer hard before she made it out.

There were three words on one line. 'All My Love'. And just below that the flamboyantly scrawled name— 'Magdalen'.

She remembered at once. The name was so distinctive. This had to be the same woman who had kept ringing here yesterday, asking for Vincent. He had looked worried when Jess mentioned it, had given Belinda a strange glance, then asked Jess hurriedly, 'You didn't tell her——?' and Jess had smiled wryly and said, 'No.'

Obviously, he hadn't wanted Magdalen to know Belinda was here. Was he afraid Magdalen would be jealous? This woman looked as if she might be quite unpleasant if she got angry. Studying her, Belinda decided she did not like that face. There was a sullen look to the overfull mouth, a hardness in the eyes, something spoilt about her.

A sound outside in the hall made her jump at that moment. She didn't want Jess to catch her being curious, so she quickly replaced the photograph, but her haste was a mistake because the piano surface was highly polished and the silver frame skidded sideways before she could catch it and fell to the floor with a horrifying tinkle of breaking glass.

'What have you done now?' an impatient voice grated from the door, and she swung round in shock, recognising Vincent's hard tones.

'Oh... I'm sorry... I... it was an accident...' She
was confused into stammering idiocy, her face flushed,
her eyes distressed.

He strode across the room, his features tight, and
picked up the photograph frame, spilling fragments of
glass which glittered on the deep-pile blue and white
carpet.

'Of course, I'll pay to have the glass replaced,' Belinda
said huskily, watching him as he stared down at the
photograph gripped by both his hands.

He didn't answer. Maybe he hadn't even heard. He
seemed totally engrossed in the image of Magdalen.
Belinda couldn't guess what he was thinking; his taut
features were masklike, his heavy lids drawn down over
those cold grey eyes. She couldn't stop staring; she was
so disturbed that her heart seemed to be in her very
throat. She ought to know this man well enough by now.
She had faced his remote contempt, stood up to his
bullying, told herself she hated and despised him. She
had thought nothing he did could ever frighten or alarm
her again, but she hated this bleak silence; it made her
want to cry.

In the end, it was she who broke the silence, her voice
a mere thread of sound. 'I'm sorry,' she almost whispered. 'I shouldn't have touched the photo, I realise that.
Honestly, it was an accident—I heard you coming and
I tried to put the photo back, but I was in too much of
a hurry, and it slipped off the piano. I... I was curious
about your girlfriend. She's very attractive, isn't she?'

'Yes,' he said, and the word was icy; it was a door
slammed in her face. He replaced the photograph then
glanced down at the glass scattered over the carpet. 'This
must be swept up immediately before someone cuts
themselves,' he said, moving away.

Belinda was getting angrier by the minute. Who did he think he was, talking to her in that tone, looking at her that way? Ever since Ricky had taken her home to meet his family she had been taking this sort of behaviour from them, and she was sick of it. Just because they had more money didn't make them any better than her, and she wasn't going to let Vincent Garrett treat her like an inferior for another second.

'She doesn't know about me, does she?' she threw at his departing back, and Vincent stopped mid-stride and swung round, his black brows together and a rapier-like sharpness in the grey eyes.

'What?'

'And you don't want her to know!' Belinda refused to let him scare her into backing off. She confronted him, her head held high and her chin up.

His eyes sliced into her viciously. 'You don't know what you're talking about.'

'Oh, yes, I do. I'm not stupid.'

'Funny, that was just the word I'd have used to describe you,' he sneered, and her face took on a harder flush.

'I heard what you said to Jess yesterday when she mentioned that this Magdalen had been ringing all day. If she knew I was here, she wouldn't like it, would she?' Belinda gave him an acid little smile, her green eyes defiant. 'She might even be jealous. That wouldn't surprise me. I expect you've given her plenty of reason not to trust you with other women. I seem to remember Ricky's laughing over your crowded love life, and what your brother knows is probably no secret from your girlfriend. Which is why you wouldn't want her to know you had driven me down here from London, or that you had visited me in hospital.'

'You're beginning to annoy me,' he snarled, and she pretended to laugh.

'Only beginning to?'

'If you've finished . . .' he snapped, half turning away.

'I haven't even started,' Belinda said. 'I've got a lot of questions to ask you first. You've been lying to me and I want the truth.'

He stiffened, eyes narrowed and glittering, then took a menacing step towards her and panic leapt into her throat, but she stood her ground and went on talking fast. At least she had his full attention now.

'For a start,' she said, 'what is this place? I was surprised to see so many photographs of your family on that piano. Why are they there? Don't tell me Jess is an old friend—that doesn't explain why the only photographs in this room are all of your family. And you said you had some sort of financial stake in this nursing home, but it isn't anything of the kind, is it? I don't know what this place is, but I do know it isn't a nursing home. There are no other patients and no staff—just Jess and that girl who does all the cooking. You lied to me, and I want to know why. What are you up to, Mr Garrett? Why have you brought me here?'

He listened without interrupting, his face expressionless, and when she came to a breathless stop he went on staring at her, still without uttering a syllable for a moment, his brows together and his mouth compressed. She picked up cold rage from him, though, and something else—uncertainty. She was puzzled by that at first, until it dawned on her that Vincent was not sure how to react to her angry accusations. Behind that blank face, his mind was working out how to deal with her. She watched him warily—would she get the truth from him even now, or was he just thinking up a new set of lies?

'OK,' he said at last, his voice quiet and smooth. 'You're right, of course. This isn't actually a nursing home, but Jess Mintern is a first-class nurse, you're in excellent hands, and you've no need to worry about anything. In fact, she was matron of a London hospital until she retired. She knows exactly what she's doing. You couldn't have better care anywhere.'

'I'm not questioning Jess's professional competence,' she said flatly. 'I like Jess, and I trust her.' She paused to eye him pointedly, and saw his mouth twist as her meaning registered. Then she went on, 'But why did you bring me here instead of taking me to a real nursing home? Come to that, what is this place and who owns it?'

'I brought you here so that I could keep an eye on you,' he drawled. 'You could make trouble for me and my family, so it made sense to put you somewhere safe for a while, and Dillingham was the most convenient place I could think of.'

A little chill hit the back of her neck. She had accused him of kidnapping her yesterday—was that precisely what he had done? Was she a prisoner?

'Whose house is this?' she whispered.

'Mine,' he said coolly, and she stared at him in silence because, although it wasn't exactly a huge surprise since she had begun to suspect it when she saw those photographs, she was dumbfounded to have him admit it with such calm assurance. There was one thing she urgently needed to know now, and she asked it in a husky voice.

'Do you mean you own it, but Jess lives here—or is this really your home?'

'I own it and I live here. Jess is an old friend of my mother's. She spent her whole working life living in rented accommodation, and when she retired she found she couldn't afford to buy a place of her own unless she sacrificed some of the things she had been looking forward to—a round-the-world cruise, for example, and six months in Australia visiting a married niece who lives there. She wanted somewhere to live and I needed a housekeeper and caretaker, so Jess took a job with me after she had been on her cruise, stopping off in Australia halfway. I'm often away, and she has the place to herself then. It's an arrangement that suits us both.'

'So everything you told me was a lie!' she said incredulously. 'You must be the biggest liar I've ever met, and I don't know if you've told me the truth, even now.'

'I have,' he said, but she glared at him.

'How can I believe that? I don't trust you an inch. If you think you're keeping me locked up here, forget it! I am leaving right now, and I'm going to make you pay for kidnapping me. There are laws in this country to punish people for doing things like that, and I'm going to make sure your girlfriend hears all about your little games, too. For her own sake, she should be told just what sort of man you really are!'

'Are you trying to blackmail me?' He closed the gap between them in a couple of strides and loomed over her, his eyes angrily mocking. 'Don't even think of it, Belinda! I'd make you sorry you ever set eyes on me!'

'I already am!' she snapped back, and regretted giving in to the impulse to retort as soon as the words left her lips and she saw the look on Vincent's hard face. She recognised that look. She had seen it yesterday just before he'd kissed her with that punitive force.

He reached for her and she instinctively put her hands against his chest to shove him away, but that contact was a physical shock. She felt something like a flash of electricity through her whole body; it burnt her nerve-ends, made her gasp, seemed to half paralyse her. The instinct to fight him off died. Belinda couldn't think. She could only stand there in dumb weakness, staring up into his intent, narrowed eyes as if hypnotised by their expression.

'You certainly ask for trouble,' Vincent said softly.

He ran a hand into her long, coppery hair and tugged her head backwards while his other hand gripped her back, pushing her closer to him. His head lowered while she stared up at him, green eyes enormous and dazed, like a rabbit transfixed by the oncoming blaze of head-lights on a dark road. That was how she felt, like some-thing helpless in the onward rush of a dark destiny. Vincent's hard mouth came nearer and nearer and she could not run away; she could not even scream out the fear possessing her.

Only as he finally took her lips did she make a sound— a wild groan that forced itself out of her and was suf-focated instantly by the hot pressure of his kiss. She wasn't touching him back or kissing him, but she made no attempt to resist; she limply allowed him to mould her closer, his hands moving sensuously from the curve of her breast to the curve of her thigh, his knee pushed against hers, his body almost merging into hers as he forced her towards him.

She was trembling violently now, appalled by the deep heat burning inside her body, shamed by the fierce jab of pleasure his mouth and hands could give her. She must stop him, before this went too far. But it had gone too far already. She hated this man—how could she let him touch her like this? What on earth was happening to her self-respect, her self-control? She had never been the sort of girl who slept around. She had been so sure that one day she would fall in love with a man who would make her happy; she had always believed in fairy-tales, trusted in love to conquer all. Well, she had certainly loved Ricky—and where had that got her? Ricky had broken her heart, and here she was in the arms of the man who had talked Ricky into betraying her. Not only was she in Vincent's arms, but he was driving her crazy with pleasure, and she loathed herself for wanting him to go on doing so.

Tears began to seep under her lids and run down her face, and Vincent must have felt them, tasted them on her skin, because he suddenly lifted his head and looked down at her, swearing hoarsely.

Belinda pulled away before he could say anything, and stumbled out of the room, sobbing incoherently as she ran up the stairs and into her bedroom. She paused long enough to lock the door before she fell on the bed, afraid that Vincent was on her heels, but she need not have feared that. He did not follow her.

She had never cried like that before; the tears seemed endless, and they did not flow the way all tears had flowed out of her before. They were wrung out of her shuddering body and they hurt unbearably; she cried in a physical convulsion of pain and thought the tears would never stop.

Vincent had shamed and shocked her. She had shamed and shocked herself. She hated him, and had the best of reasons for doing so, and yet she had trembled in his arms, wanting him with desperation. He had given her more pleasure than any man, even Ricky, had ever done. She had never wanted anyone the way she had wanted Vincent a few moments ago. She felt sick at the very memory of how she had felt in his arms, but the bitter truth was that if Vincent had wanted to he could have got her into bed just now. She had been helpless to say no to him. If he had pushed her down on to the floor and made love to her there and then, in that room, he could have taken her without any resistance.

Her tears at last dried up and she lay on the bed, face down, trembling and fighting to get back some semblance of normality. She had to pull herself together. Any minute now, Jess might knock on the door to find out what was wrong, and how could she face her in this state?

She forced herself on to her feet and splashed cold water on her face. In the mirror her eyes stared back looking very unfamiliar: lids puffy, reddened, her lashes tear-drenched, her face shadowed and pale.

Her eyes held something more—an agony of shame and bewilderment. They questioned her. Why? Why did you let it happen? Why did you let him do that to you? What is the matter with you?

She couldn't understand herself any more. She didn't recognise herself. Her behaviour was so inexplicable, so disturbing—why had she let a man she hated and despised make love to her?

Why? She stared into her tortured eyes and suddenly her skin seemed to freeze to her bones. There was, after all, one obvious explanation of all this.

It could be a legacy of her coma. Had she suffered brain damage, after all? She was acting unpredictably, doing stupid things, puzzling things, losing control of herself. Was she going crazy?

CHAPTER FIVE

IT WAS half an hour before Belinda could face unlocking her door, and by then she was looking almost normal, her hair brushed, her clothes neat, her face wearing make-up that hid the ravages of her tears. Nobody had knocked on her door, so either Jess hadn't missed her or Vincent Garrett had warned her against going upstairs to find out why she was in her room. But what on earth could he say? she thought, then a bitter humour made her grimace. That would be no problem, he would lie, of course. What else did he ever do?

She would do a little lying herself. She looked for a paperback of one of her favourite books, *Jane Eyre*, which one of the nurses had given her as a farewell present. It would make a good excuse for having gone back to her room.

When she went downstairs again she met Jess in the hall. 'Oh, there you are!' said Jess cheerfully, but Belinda felt she was being given a thoughtful, probing look, from which she half turned her head so that Jess only got her profile.

'I was just looking for this!' she said, holding up her book.

'Oh, you've got something to read! I was going to offer you some magazines. I thought you might like to sit in the garden this morning so I've put a chair out on the lawn; you can read out there in the sun,' Jess told her, and Belinda eagerly accepted.

She was unlikely to have any trouble from Vincent Garrett out there, in full view of the house, and it would give her time alone, to think. Jess took her out there, saw her settled in the deep-cushioned wicker chair, with a white and green striped garden umbrella arranged to keep the sun off her face, and a low wicker table beside her, on which Jess had arranged a jug of iced lemonade, a glass, and a little plate of biscuits.

Looking at them, Belinda grinned. 'Are you trying to fatten me up?'

Jess just laughed. 'If you want me, ring this.' She pointed to the little brass bell on the table and then she went back to the house.

Belinda sat back, her book open on her lap, pretending to read. Her mind was hunting feverishly for a way out of the trap Vincent had laid for her.

She had to get away from here; she couldn't stay in this house. She never wanted to see him again. She didn't yet know his precise intentions, but she suspected they were not good. What had he said? That he wanted her somewhere 'safe'? What did that mean? A shiver ran down her spine. She didn't trust him or like him.

But even if she could escape where was she to go? She had no home now, and her mother was on the other side of the world. She had some money in the bank, of course. She could go to a hotel, or find herself a new flat, but she knew she wasn't yet over the effects of her injuries. She still had dizzy spells from time to time, she often felt tired or weak, and she got headaches, although they were no longer such bad ones, and they came more and more rarely.

It would be dangerous to be alone, though, or not to have immediate medical help on hand. That was the whole idea of going to a convalescent home. Perhaps she could go back to the hospital and ask them to find her a real convalescent home?

A little flush crept up her face at the idea of explaining. What could she say, for heaven's sake? It would be so embarrassing, it would make her sound crazy...

She closed her eyes, flinching. I'm not. I am not crazy. I mustn't let myself think such a thing. Vincent Garrett would like me to believe it, no doubt. He wants to undermine me, destroy my self-confidence, stop me suing his brother for a fortune. That is what this is all about. Money. He is determined not to give me any money, if he can help it, and he is ready to use any weapon that comes to hand. Even sex.

Her stomach churned. She couldn't bear to remember herself in his arms; she hated the very thought of how she had felt during those few moments.

He's unscrupulous, an opportunist, she thought, her face hardening. She looked up and stared across the garden at a white rose in bloom, but did not really see it at all. Instead, she saw a dark, ruthless face, and her hands screwed into fists on her lap. She had to get away from him, away from here.

She could ring her mother and say she was coming to New Zealand, then book a flight and just go. How could he stop her?

There was a phone in her room, and Jess had promised she could ring her mother. She would do that later today. As soon as she had talked to her mother, she would book the first possible flight, then she would pack and ring for a taxi and spend a night in a hotel near the airport.

It was all very simple, really, after all, and she leaned back with a sigh, suddenly very tired. She had been getting worked up over nothing. Vincent Garrett wasn't superhuman; he had no power over her. She only had to put her mind to it and she could walk away from him, and he would not be able to stop her, short of using physical force, and even he wouldn't do that. Why had she let herself get into such a state over him?

She closed her eyes again, and drifted into half-sleep, the sun warm on her arms and legs, but the cool shade of the umbrella protecting her face, and the air fresh and sweet with the scent of roses.

'Lunch is ready,' a voice said, and she woke with a start to find Jess beside her looking amused. 'You've been asleep for an hour!'

'I haven't!' Belinda guiltily looked at her watch, and it was true. She made a face. 'I just dozed off, after sleeping for hours last night, too—how dreadful!'

'You obviously need the sleep, and it will have done you a power of good to be out here in the fresh air.'

Belinda followed her back into the house. There was no sign of Vincent. She ate her lunch with Jess in the room where she had eaten her breakfast. It was a simple meal: soup followed by a salad with steak and after that some fresh fruit salad. They drank mineral water with it and had coffee, then Jess insisted that she take another rest, this time in her room, on her bed, for an hour.

'Then I think you should do your remedial exercises and have some massage,' she said. 'From tomorrow we'll start a proper routine, working morning and afternoon on strengthening those muscles, but as this is your first day here I thought we would go easy on you.'

'Well, thank you,' Belinda said, feeling guilty because Jess was so kind and friendly. When she was alone in her room she would ring her mother and then the airline, and soon she would have gone, but she couldn't tell Jess that because Jess would obviously tell Vincent, and she could not risk that.

But when she dialled her mother's number, some ten minutes later, there was no reply. Belinda looked at her watch, surprised, then tried again. Still no answer.

She lay down and closed her eyes, but this time sleep would not come, so she read *Jane Eyre*, thinking to escape into another world, only to find Vincent's dark face intruding on every page. She closed the book and chose another, a detective story this time. It held her attention without reminding her of things she preferred to forget, and she was still reading it when Jess knocked on her door.

'Time for exercises!'

'Thank heavens for that! I was getting very bored. Isn't it odd? I slept this morning, when I wasn't supposed to, then when I lay down on the bed this afternoon I couldn't so much as doze.'

Jess laughed. 'That's normal, don't worry. Just relax and take things as they come. You'll sleep when you need it, and if you can't—well, just lying down and resting will do you good. Now, what do you wear when you're doing your exercises?'

'I've got a leotard; shall I put it on?'

'Yes, and come downstairs. There's a gym in the basement. I'll show you round and then you can use the equipment whenever you feel like it. There's an indoor swimming-pool, too. After your exercises you can have a swim, if you like, or use the sauna.'

'Mr Garrett has it all, doesn't he?' Belinda said drily, and Jess gave her a quick look.

'So you know it's his house, then? Whatever gave you the idea it was a nursing home? Well, I suppose everything must be very strange to you for the moment. You've been through a bad experience, so you must expect to have trouble getting back to normal, but, as I said, take it slowly and everything will be just fine.'

She thinks I'm crazy, too, Belinda thought bleakly, staring at her kind, lined face.

'Where's your leotard?' asked Jess. 'Can I help you get into it?'

'No, I can manage, I don't need your help!' Belinda said sharply. Did Jess think she was incapable even of dressing herself?

'Well, then, I'll see you downstairs.' Jess spoke gently, recognising that she had upset Belinda. She went, and Belinda found her leotard and put it on with jerky, hurried fingers, frowning at her reflection in the mirror.

Her green eyes were disturbed. What is wrong with me? Why did I snap at Jess like that? Jess is sorry for me, she tries to soothe me, but she thinks I came out of that coma only half there. Maybe I did? I certainly don't feel the same as the girl who was in that car before it crashed. My mind works differently; I see the world in a new way. Surely I was never so full of anger and violent emotion one minute, then weary and dull the next?

I'm sure I was quite a level-tempered person. I don't remember these shifting moods, these sudden surges of anger or the flatness afterwards. I thought I was more or less back to normal when they let me leave hospital, but perhaps I'm nothing of the kind.

Nobody tells you the truth, that's the trouble. Who do I ask? Who will tell me if I'm unbalanced since I came out of the coma? Jess? The specialist at the hospital?

Vincent? The name came unprompted, and was rejected at once with another of those flares of pure burning rage. Vincent Garrett? She laughed angrily. Vincent Garrett would lie to her, just as he always did.

He was her enemy, she must never forget that; she could not trust him. If she asked him what time it was, he would be just as likely to lie, if it suited him.

Jess took her through her remedial exercises slowly, to get some idea of how she was progressing. 'We won't push it as this is our first day,' she said, after half an hour. 'Now I'll give you some massage, then you can have a swim.'

The pool was situated in a dome-roofed building, a floor up from the gymnasium, which had once been a conservatory, Jess said. The water was heated and impossibly blue; there were loungers set out on the tiled floor so that you could relax after swimming, and there was a sauna cubicle at one side of the pool, but Belinda decided not to bother taking a sauna that afternoon. She preferred to swim; Jess agreed.

They swam together. Belinda realised that Jess was wary of leaving her alone in the pool; it was another indication that Jess had her doubts about her condition, and indeed Belinda found the brief swim tiring, and was not sorry to get out of the water.

'You're bound to feel some strain in exercise, at first,' Jess said kindly. 'Take it slow and steady, a little every day, building up gradually—that's the idea, and in a month you'll be amazed by the difference. This is why the hospital advised a long convalescence. You just aren't going to be able to go back to normal life for a long time, my dear, but if you're patient and work at it you will get there, I promise you.'

Belinda towelled herself, put on a warm, fluffy towelling robe, and went back to her room to dress. On the landing, she walked straight into Vincent Garrett.

Her body jerked in shock. She froze on the spot, looking at him with wide, frightened green eyes, and

Vincent Garrett stared back at her, his black brows drawn and his face taut.

'Don't look at me like that! I'm sorry I made you cry; I didn't intend to upset you like that.'

She just stared at him, eyes accusing, and he scowled.

'If you're trying to make me feel guilty you're doing a great job of it.'

'Good!' she said, clutching the lapels of her robe and holding them together, to hide the glimpse of her breasts they might otherwise give him.

He didn't miss the gesture, and a dark red colour crawled up his face. 'You don't need to act as if I were Jack the Ripper. I'm not going to touch you again. I lost my temper earlier. You made me furious, or I'd never have laid a hand on you.'

'Am I supposed to find that reassuring?' Belinda asked coldly. 'What's to stop you doing it again? You have one of the worst tempers I've ever met.'

'Try not to provoke me, then!' he said through his teeth, eyeing her with dislike.

'Oh, of course, it was all my fault! It would be, wouldn't it? It couldn't possibly be you who was to blame.'

'You shouldn't have tried to blackmail me!'

'You shouldn't have brought me here under false pretences!'

They stared at each other, both flushed, both bristling with anger, then Vincent laughed shortly.

'Talking to you is like playing chess. I suppose we've reached stalemate. Do we have to go on like this, shrieking accusations and threats at each other? It's getting very tiresome. Can't we call a truce?'

She stared at him, one hand gripping the lapels of her robe, the other clenched at her side in a fist.

He stepped closer, smiling in a coaxing fashion, his grey eyes gleaming. 'Look, you're still very frail, Belinda. This perpetual squabbling isn't doing you any good, and I can do without it myself. While you're here under this roof, could we have a little peaceful co-existence, do you think?'

He didn't know that she was planning to leave here very soon, but the thought was in her mind as she listened, frowning. Well, why not? she thought. At least it would put him off his guard—he wouldn't be expecting her to escape if they had a truce.

She deliberately relaxed, let her clenched hand open, held it out with a curt nod. 'OK. A truce, for the time being.'

'Thank you.' He studied her, took her hand and held it, staring down at her, making her uneasy. 'Your hair curls naturally, then,' he said oddly, and she blinked.

'What?'

He touched her wet, tangled, coppery hair lightly with his other hand. 'In fact, it's curlier now than it is when it's dry.'

She was breathing far too fast; it must be the effect of the exercise and then the swimming.

'Yes, I must go and dry it,' she said huskily, ultra-conscious of the fact that he was still holding her hand. She tugged at her imprisoned fingers and he let go of them. Belinda gave him a nervous little smile, then turned and hurried into her bedroom, locking the door behind her before she felt able to relax.

She had dinner with both Jess and Vincent, and afterwards they all sat listening to a concert on the radio. The music was gentle and calm; she relaxed, listening. She had been through a great deal since she'd arrived in this house; she needed a little peace.

It was the first time that she had ever been in Vincent's company without quarrelling with him. She watched him warily whenever he wasn't looking her way, trying to read character into the familiar façade of his face, but he still puzzled her. One thing was clear: Jess liked him, and he was invariably nice to Jess, but then, she thought cynically, he could afford to be nice to Jess. She was no threat to him; she wouldn't be suing him for a lot of money, and he hadn't done Jess a bitter injury.

It was a truism that people always hated those they had wronged, even if they were prepared to forgive anyone who wronged them. Vincent knew he had hurt her badly. No wonder he flew into a rage every time he came near her.

Vincent had left a newspaper on the table beside her, and she registered the headlines vaguely as she was listening to the music, then noted the date with another of those jabs of shock which came whenever she realised that she had lost eight months of her life. For her, time had stopped. Everyone else had got on with their lives, including Ricky. How could she help being bitter when she kept remembering that?

'I think I'll go to bed now,' she said, as the music ended.

'Would you like some hot milk or cocoa when you're in bed? I'm making myself some,' Jess said.

'If it's no trouble, yes, please. Cocoa would be lovely.'

'I'll bring it up,' Jess promised, and Vincent stood up as they both left the room.

'Goodnight, Belinda,' he said quietly.

'Goodnight,' she said in the same tone.

She fell asleep as soon as her head touched the pillow, and in the morning Jess teased her about it. 'I found you dead to the world, so I put out your light and tiptoed

out again with the cocoa. You must have been exhausted! I think you had better take it easy for a few days.
Coming out of hospital after such a long time is quite
a strain, my dear.'

Belinda frowned. 'Do you think I'd be up to a long
journey? How soon could I fly out to New Zealand, for
instance?'

Jess made a face. 'Not for quite a few weeks, I'm
afraid. Is this to join your family?'

Belinda nodded, and Jess gave her a thoughtful look.
'Well, I wouldn't advise it just yet, anyway. Wait until
you are stronger. And, in the meantime, work at your
exercises and take daily walks. You have a lot of muscle
wastage to make up, you know.'

Belinda rang her mother later that morning. It was,
of necessity, a brief conversation because of the cost of
such a long-distance call, and Belinda found it a frus-
trating experience because the line was bad and half her
mother's words were swallowed up in a roaring noise,
but it was good to hear her mother's voice and she rang
off feeling better. 'I'm coming to New Zealand as soon
as I'm fit enough to travel,' she promised. 'Bye, see you
soon!'

Her mother's voice echoed back, 'See you soon,
darling!'

'Ready to do some exercises now?' Jess asked her,
smiling, as Belinda came back downstairs wearing her
black leotard.

The days fell into a pattern very rapidly; exercise, food,
and rest—they were all life meant for a while. It was
peaceful, and dull. She saw Vincent in the evenings, after
work, and at the weekend, although he led, she realised,
a busy social life and was often out. When they did meet,
she kept up a polite façade, and so did Vincent, both of

them aware that if they quarrelled life could be very un-comfortable since they had to live under one roof for the moment.

It was a couple of weekends later that Vincent surprised her by walking into her bedroom at night when she was almost asleep.

She sat up, looking at him in confusion. He was carrying a tray in his hand and grinned at her.

'Here you are—your cocoa. I brought it up because Jess spilt the milk as she was pouring it out, so she's busy mopping up in the kitchen.'

'Oh, dear, poor Jess,' Belinda said, avoiding meeting his eyes.

'She said you mustn't let it get cold or it will be un-drinkable. She sent some biscuits, too.'

'She thinks I'm too skinny.' Belinda's throat was dry, and she could hardly speak, she was so nervous about having him in her room.

'You are very thin,' he agreed calmly as he set the tray down on her bedside table, his narrowed grey gaze wandering over her in the simple little green cotton nightdress, with its scooped neckline and short puff sleeves. 'You look like a little girl in that,' he said.

She gave a husky laugh. 'Thanks!' There was something oddly reassuring in the comment, though. It made her less uptight. Or was that what he had intended? She bit down on her inner lip. She really must stop looking behind his every remark, seeing shadows in every corner.

'Sunday tomorrow,' he said. 'You haven't been out of the house since you got here. How would you like to go for a drive? Jess says you're up to it now. She thought we could drive, then have lunch in the country.'

'That sounds wonderful,' she said in startled spontaneity, because it was so long since she had done any-

thing like that. Like the Lady of Shalott, she had been
living remote from everyday life, viewing the world as
if in a looking-glass. She longed to break out. 'I'd love
to. Jess is so thoughtful!'

Vincent smiled down into her eyes, as if he understood what she was thinking, and sympathised, and her
traitorous heart missed a beat.

'I thought it was time you had some fun again,' he
said gently. 'Well, goodnight, and sleep well.'

The door closed behind him and Belinda sat up in the
bed staring at where he had been, as if still seeing him,
her green eyes enormous, one finger winding a strand
of coppery hair round and round in blank stupefaction.
That smile had left her breathless.

For the first time she could really understand why
other women apparently found him fascinating. He had
never looked at her like that before, but she knew she
would never forget that smile—the revelation of a very
different man behind the icy, hostile façade she knew so
well.

By the time she drank her cocoa it was only lukewarm,
but that didn't matter. She lay down and tried to sleep,
but all she could think about was Vincent's grey eyes
with a smile in them, the lazy warmth of his mouth. It
was a long time before she did fall asleep, and she woke
up early, getting up at once to pull aside the curtain and
check on the weather. If it was raining she knew they
wouldn't go, and she was on tenterhooks until she looked
out and saw the summer morning.

A heat haze hung over the distant countryside; the sky
was blue and the grass glistened with dew. It was going
to be a marvellous day.

She showered and dressed in a light, summer dress of
cool cotton, a simple tunic style, quite short, showing

her slender legs up to the knee. The colour suited her, a golden shade which accented her green eyes and brightened her copper hair.

Vincent wasn't around when she went downstairs, and Jess was amused by her impatience for him to put in an appearance. 'He never gets up before ten on a Sunday, and he won't be leaving for ages.'

In fact, it was half-past eleven before Vincent arrived, and Belinda met him with an eager smile. 'When are we going?'

He gave her a teasing look. 'No rush, is there?'

'Yes! I'm dying to go!' Noticing the slow appraisal of his grey eyes, she asked anxiously, 'Is my dress OK?'

'It's delightful,' he drawled. 'I hadn't realised what gorgeously long legs you have.' She turned pink and was relieved when he coolly went on, 'But that sun is quite hot; I think you should wear a hat.'

'I don't have one. I never wear them.'

'Well, you aren't going out with me in this heat without a hat on your head. I don't want you collapsing with sunstroke. Wait here.' He vanished and came back with a wide-brimmed white straw hat with a pale green ribbon around the crown. 'Try this!' he ordered.

'Whose is it?' she said uncertainly, taking the hat and admiring it, while not sure she had the nerve to wear it. Hats made her uneasy.

'My sister left it here after she stayed with me last summer. Here, let me.' He took it from her again and put it on her head, stood back to survey her and adjusted it. 'Perfect,' he murmured. 'Well, let's go, then, as you're in such a tearing hurry!'

As they left the house, Belinda noted with quick, furtive, sidelong glances what he was wearing—summer clothes, like herself: a crisp white shirt, blue silk tie, dark

blue trousers, and a blue-striped white linen jacket which
gave him a very continental air. He hadn't bought that
in Savile Row, she thought wryly. It had the unmis-
takable stamp of a French designer—cool, casual chic.
On Vincent it surprised, yet there was no question but
that it suited him.

It was only as Vincent started the car that Belinda realised that someone was missing. 'Wait...where's Jess?'
she burst out, frowning.

'She decided not to come,' he said casually, and the
car shot away.

'Why not?' Belinda pressed, alarmed. She had been
expecting a safe, comfortable threesome, and the
prospect of hours in Vincent's exclusive company left
her decidedly on edge. 'I thought it was her idea! What
changed her mind?'

He shrugged, and gave her a drily reproachful look.
'She probably felt like having some time to herself.'

Belinda flushed, at once feeling mean and selfish,
which was probably what he'd intended, but guessing
that did not make any difference. 'Oh. O-of course,' she
stammered. 'She works so hard, she deserves a break.'

A little silence fell as he drove on, his eyes on the
road, his long, brown fingers lightly resting on the wheel.

'Anyway, you're not scared of being alone with me,
are you, Belinda?' he asked in a soft, mocking voice
that made her tense and look away, her mouth dry.

'Scared? Certainly not!' she at once denied, and heard
him laugh quietly.

'Oh, good!'

Belinda bit her lip, her hands woven together in her
lap, fingers tense and clenched. Vincent was in a dangerous mood; she must keep her wits about her if she was

to survive the ordeal of being alone with him for hours on end.

'Where are we going?' she asked, and he told her that he was making for a charming little country hotel beside a river.

'The food is simple but very good, and it's never crowded because there are only eight tables in the place. The people who run it like to keep things small and easy to run. They're a young married couple; Bridie and Sean Stevens. You'll like them.'

Belinda was ready not to like them, since they were apparently friends of Vincent's, but in fact he was right—she took to them on sight. They were in their early twenties, energetic, good-humoured, and interested in everyone in the little restaurant. Bridie had short, tidy fair hair and round, pale blue eyes. Sean was skinny and dark with liquid brown eyes.

They greeted Vincent warmly, Bridie hugging him, Sean grinning and shaking hands. When Vincent introduced Belinda she met two pairs of curious, friendly eyes while she shook hands.

'Your taste is as good as ever,' Sean said aside to Vincent, winking at him.

'That sounds terrible, Sean!' said Bridie, and to Belinda said, 'Take no notice of my husband; that was meant as a joke.'

'It was meant as a compliment!' said Sean. 'And I'm sure Belinda knows that she isn't exactly the first woman in Vincent's life, but does she know that she's the first one he has ever brought here? He must be serious.'

They both looked at Vincent, laughing. Belinda was tense and flushed, her eyes lowered, but she still picked up the vibrations of Vincent's irritation. He wasn't amused. 'You've got it wrong,' he said shortly. 'Belinda isn't my girlfriend. She's just——' He broke off, his brows corrugated, and Sean grinned, encouraging him with teasing disbelief.

'Yes? She's what? Your aunt? Your secretary? Your chaperon? What?'

'Oh, go and get us a drink!' he said, scowling.

Bridie patted his arm. 'Poor Vincent. Stop it, Sean, you know he hates being teased.'

'No sense of humour, that's his trouble. I'm off back to my kitchen before the lunch burns. See you later, you two. I hope you enjoy the food, Belinda.'

Bridie watched her husband dart away, very small and slight in his enveloping white apron and white chef's hat, and her eyes had affection in them. Then she looked back at Vincent. 'Sorry about that, Vincent. Sean has a weird idea of fun. Now, what would you like to drink?'

'Just a tomato juice for me,' Belinda said.

'Make that two,' said Vincent. 'I have to drive back after lunch, and we'll probably be having wine with the food, so I must watch my intake.'

'Sure,' said Bridie, and showed them to a table, handing them each a menu. 'The drinks won't be a minute.'

The hotel was Jacobean, black-beamed and white-plastered with low ceilings and leaded windows which looked out directly on to the river flowing past between green banks of grass and drooping willow which made a delightful shade on such a hot summer day. The restaurant was a long, narrow room taking up one side of the ground floor, and containing just eight tables, five of them only big enough for two people, the white damask cloths laid elegantly with silverware and good glass, a slim silver vase holding just two dark red roses on each.

Belinda was aware of curious gazes from some of the other guests—no doubt Vincent was well known here and people were wondering exactly who she was—but she did not return the staring. She kept her eyes on the menu, which was, as Vincent had warned her, limited. Today there was just a choice between starters of asparagus soup or melon filled with fresh fruit, followed by either a whole roast poussin in tarragon and mushroom sauce, or salmon trout served with dill and almonds.

'I'll have the soup and then chicken,' Vincent decided, and Belinda chose melon and trout because she did not feel hungry. She was too much on edge, her stomach was full of butterflies, and whenever she looked in Vincent's direction she felt extremely odd.

What is the matter with me? I don't even like him. I have every reason to hate the man. Why am I feeling this way?

Bridie brought their tomato juice and took their order. When they were alone again, Belinda became increasingly conscious of the man sitting opposite her, and that was disturbing. The first course arrived; she concentrated on her melon so that she didn't have to talk to Vincent. He seemed unaware of her silence; he talked quietly about this and that: the dark oak furniture, matching the period of the building, the Jacobean prints hanging on the walls. He asked if she was enjoying her melon, said that his soup was delicious. Forced to say something, she asked huskily where Sean and Bridie had learnt their jobs when Bridie came to bring them their second course.

'Oh, I went to catering college, but Sean was born into the business. His family had a hotel in Ireland in Tipperary, near Clonmel. If you're ever that way, drop in—it's well worth a visit.'

'I'll remember that,' Belinda said, still avoiding Vincent's eyes. The trout was as good as the melon had been, and she only wished she had more appetite, but she managed to eat most of it. When Bridie suggested a dessert, though, she ruefully said no.

'I really couldn't eat another thing. I'll just have coffee.'

'So will I,' Vincent said. 'That poussin was almost a full-grown chicken!'

Bridie laughed. 'Go on with you! OK, coffee for two—do you want it here, or in the lounge?'

'Why not in the lounge?' Vincent shrugged, looking at Belinda. 'Is that fine with you?'

'Yes, thank you.'

He rose and Belinda followed him out of the restaurant into the hotel lounge, which was scattered with deep armchairs and low tables on which were placed magazines and newspapers. There were flowers here and there, and fringed table lamps; the atmosphere was comfortable and homely.

Vincent chose chairs by the window, but as he walked towards them Belinda realised she had to get away for a few moments, so she excused herself and went to the powder-room, where she sat down in front of a mirror, her elbows on the table, her head propped on her hands, staring at her own reflection.

What is happening to me? she asked herself, then she saw the door opening and couldn't face having to talk to anyone, so went into one of the pink-doored cubicles to wait until the new arrivals had gone. She could hear them talking as they renewed their make-up; middle-aged voices, she decided, gossipy and just the slightest bit tipsy after the wine at lunch, no doubt.

'Oh, the food is always good,' one woman said, with pauses between words as she applied lipstick. 'But it's such a small place. You're cheek by jowl with everyone else, and people do eavesdrop dreadfully. That woman at the next table to us, the one in the extraordinary yellow hat—she didn't miss a word we said, did you notice?'

'You can't help it, sometimes,' said the other voice. 'I wasn't trying to listen, but I kept picking up what Vincent Garrett was saying.'

'Was it anything exciting?' the first one asked avidly.

'Not really, but my goodness he is good-looking, isn't he? Much better-looking than that brother of his, the one who got married not long ago. I remember the wedding photos in the country magazine. What is his name?'

'Richard. I know their mother quite well, you know. Oh, yes, we've served on various charity committees together. I prefer Richard, myself. A bit young for me, of course, but I always did like blond men.'

'Really, Judith!' The other woman chuckled, though. 'Does Tom know? I'm shocked.'

'Get away with you! I'm twice his age, but I can look, can't I? What I say is, men always do—however old they are, they like to give a pretty girl a sideways look—so why shouldn't women? Come on, Marion, you fancy Vincent, admit it! Mind you, so does the girl with him! She wasn't bad-looking, either, but a bit skinny, I thought.'

'Lucky girl,' sighed the second woman. 'Oh, I must go on a diet. I wonder if his brother's getting married has put ideas into Vincent's head. One marriage in a family often leads to others.'

'Vincent is a tough bird to catch, though. He's had years of practice in evading predatory women, and I'm not sure Richard is a good example. I saw him the other day in Aylesbury and he didn't look what you could call radiant. In fact, he looked fed up to me.'

Belinda felt as if she had been punched in the stomach. She leaned on the wall of the cubicle, listening with terrible intensity, her face white, her eyes huge. Ricky was back from his honeymoon. He was in England again, and he didn't seem happy.

'Always the way with young marrieds, isn't it? They think it's going to be bliss forever, and then reality breaks in and they find out that it isn't as easy living with someone as they had expected.'

'And if it isn't perfect at once they just get a divorce! Young people won't work at it, the way we used to have to...'

The door opened and swished shut, the voices trailed away and silence fell in the little powder-room. Belinda slowly emerged and stood staring at her reflection in the mirror.

Her eyes held a confused swirl of emotions. If Ricky's marriage wasn't working out, was it because he still cared for her? His family had rushed him into that marriage. Perhaps he had still been reluctant, perhaps he had believed she would never recover and so he hadn't cared what happened. How could a marriage based on such a foundation ever work?

A thought hit her and made her bite her lip, her eyes very wide and unsure. Did Ricky know she had recovered consciousness, was out of hospital? He must do; his family couldn't keep the news from him forever. Or could they? Vincent was capable of anything, however devious, to get his own way.

When Ricky did find out, wouldn't he come to find her, though? She took a long, painful breath, her body tense.

And when she did see him again, how was she going to feel? Did she still love him, or had her feelings changed since she'd recovered consciousness to find that he had married someone else? She had been as bitter as death at first; she had hated him almost as much as she hated his brother, but slowly, imperceptibly, she realised, the picture had changed in her head, the kaleidoscope had shifted, and the pattern she saw now was quite different. If she was to be honest, she couldn't blame Ricky for letting himself be stampeded into abandoning her. The accident had been a shock, and her long coma must have been even more traumatic. Poor Ricky wasn't the type of man to stand up to such an experience very well. He was a spoilt younger son, born to sunshine and optimism. Grief was something he hadn't met before. He wouldn't have known how to deal with it. It was typical of him to flee, to take the easier road.

A rueful smile tugged at her mouth, as she remembered him—the quick, easy smile, the golden certainty. No, Ricky was not cut from the same tough, impervious material as his older brother.

None of which answered her question—how did she feel about Ricky now and, if he came, how would she react?

CHAPTER SIX

VINCENT was sipping his coffee when Belinda returned, and looked sharply at her, a frown between his dark brows. 'I was about to organise a search party. You've been gone so long that I thought you might have walked out on me. Aren't you feeling well?'

She sat down and stared back at him with open, aggressive hostility. 'Why didn't you tell me Ricky was back?'

He drew an audible breath, his eyes narrowing. 'Who told you?'

'I overheard some women in the powder-room talking about you and Ricky. They mentioned his wedding, and one of them said he was back from his honeymoon—she had seen him in Aylesbury the other day.'

Vincent's face was taut and yet oddly blank, his eyes had a veiled opacity, as if he was listening very intently and thinking hard, but fighting not to let her glimpse anything that was in his mind.

'So,' he said slowly, 'that's why you were gone so long! What were you doing—eavesdropping, or gossiping?'

The deliberate jab made her angrier. 'Don't be so insulting! I couldn't help overhearing what they were saying, could I? I was in there when they came in, and I had no idea they were going to talk about Ricky, but I certainly didn't speak to them. I wasn't doing any of the gossiping. And don't try to change the subject, or side-track me—just answer my question. Why didn't you tell me Ricky was back in England?'

He shrugged, talking smoothly. 'Ricky's a married man now, he has a wife and a new life with her. Everything else is in the past and must be forgotten. I thought his whereabouts were no concern of yours.'

One part of her mind admitted that what he had said was mere common sense—Ricky was married and there was no going back from that—yet at the same time she was so angry with Vincent for keeping things from her, for treating her as if she were a child with no right to be told the truth, or make her own decisions.

Fiercely, she burst out, 'You mean, you didn't want me to know he was back in case I tried to see him, in case I upset your cosy little family apple-cart!'

Vincent stared fixedly at her, his lean features tight and shadowed.

'You aren't going to see him!' he said sharply. 'Ricky is married, get that through your head. He is out of your life for good. He has a wife who loves him——'

'And I didn't?' she interrupted with bitter force, and his grey eyes flashed like savage lightning.

'I'm glad to see you're using the past tense.'

Her whole body tensed in shock. She had used the past tense; she hadn't noticed it as the words came out— but was her love for Ricky over? Was it all in the past? Or had those words burst out of her in such rage that she wasn't even thinking what she was saying? If she didn't still care for Ricky, why was she so upset at hearing he was back in England and probably only a few miles away from her at this very moment? It might have been she who had walked into him in Aylesbury! How would she feel if she did see him? That was the question for which she had no answer.

Vincent was watching her closely; Belinda had the distinct feeling that he was trying to read her face and she carefully shuttered it, hiding her thoughts from him.

Quietly, he added, 'Oh, you may have thought you loved him once, but it is over now. He's gone. Forget him.' He waited for her to answer, but she didn't speak, so at last he drew a long breath, leaned over and picked up the silver coffee-pot. 'Now, can I pour your coffee? You like it with cream and sugar, don't you?'

She was still seething with chaotic emotion, but she deliberately reined it all in and nodded without speaking, because on one level she could see the sense of what he said and she wanted time to think. She would tell him what she thought of him on some other occasion.

Vincent poured her coffee, added sugar and cream, then stirred it for her—again, as if she were a child, she thought, watching. He was a man used to managing, dictating, commanding. He organised other people's lives for them and thought nothing of it. It didn't seem to occur to him that some people might not want their lives run for them by someone else; that some people might prefer to make their own decisions, choose their own futures, even stir their own coffee.

'Here you are!' he said then, holding out her cup, his face wearing one of those smiles of his which she knew were meant to coax and charm.

He really was an infuriating man, and she wished she still found it so easy to dislike him. Hatred was something else; she could manage that whenever she remembered what he and his family had done to her life, but it was something of a shock to discover that you could hate someone and yet feel a grudging liking for them. Belinda hadn't yet worked out how that could happen, and it bothered her.

Impatient with herself for being so stupidly complicated, she took the cup from him and their fingers
brushed, sending a strange, angry shiver through her.

Fortunately, he was quite unaware of how the brief
contact had affected her. 'Drink your coffee while it's
still hot,' he ordered, and she eyed him sideways, her
face wry.

'Yes, sir! Your wish is my command!'

He gave her a quick glance, then mockery filled his
eyes. 'What a touchy creature you are. Why can't you
see that I'm giving you very good advice?'

He was not talking about her coffee, but she pretended not to realise that.

'All right! I'm drinking it,' she said and took a sip.
Vincent finished his own and took another cup, then re-
filled hers just as Sean and Bridie emerged from the restaurant to join them. Sean had shed his chef's clothes;
he was in jeans and a bright green T-shirt now and looked
even younger.

'A wonderful meal! You are a great cook,' Belinda
congratulated him, and he looked very pleased.

'I'm glad you enjoyed it. Nothing so ghastly as
cooking for people who do nothing but complain
afterwards!'

'An artist likes to be appreciated,' Bridie said in mock
solemnity, and Sean grinned at her.

'You may be joking, but it's absolutely true. Knowing
your work is appreciated is half the motive for working
at all.' He glanced at the window, sighing. 'Why else
should any sane man slave over a hot stove in a steamy
kitchen for hours when he could be outside enjoying a
day like this? What glorious weather, isn't it?'

'Yes, lovely,' said Belinda, smiling back at him. 'And
I'd swear I just heard a cuckoo calling somewhere on

the other bank of the river. The first cuckoo I've heard this year. Isn't it strange how nostalgic it is to hear a cuckoo? No other bird has quite that effect.'

Sean nodded at her in agreement. 'We first hear them in May, usually. There's a little copse over there; every year the cuckoos come back to it, and on a fine Monday, when we're closed, we sometimes take a picnic basket and go over in the boat for a few hours. Lounge on the grass under the trees and listen to the cuckoo. Funny how you can never work out exactly where the little devil is!'

'I was thinking of taking out a boat for an hour. I thought it would be rather pleasant on the river this afternoon,' Vincent said idly, and Sean at once offered to let them borrow his boat.

'It's only a small rowing-boat, but if you chuck a few cushions into it you can make it quite comfortable.'

'Do you row, Vincent?' Bridie asked, and Sean gave a great roar of laughter.

'Woman, you don't know what you've said! This man is an Oxford rowing blue.'

Bridie grinned at Belinda. 'Aren't men's tribal customs quaint? I often wonder if they ever grow up at all, the little dears.'

'Take no notice of her, Belinda,' Vincent said smilingly. 'Would you like an hour on the river?'

'With you doing all the work?' she said with dulcet sweetness. 'I'd love it.'

Bridie laughed. 'She got you there, Vincent!'

'Typical female attitude,' Sean said. 'That's their great plan in life—to get a man to work for them while they loll back on a pile of cushions. Talking of which, let's grab a few cushions, and we'll take you down to see the boat.'

Bridie went around the lounge, gathering up a handful of the older cushions from the deep armchairs, then they all went down through the garden to a small boathouse right on the river, where Sean proudly showed them his little fleet of boats.

He had one for every occasion, it seemed: a well-used but recently revarnished rowing-boat, a small dinghy and a fair-sized sea-going yacht with the name *Bridie Two* painted along the side.

'No motorboat?' Belinda asked innocently and the other three all looked at her in apparent horror.

'Good heavens, no!' said Sean, appalled at the very idea. 'I hate the damned things. They make a racket, they stink, and they deposit oil in the river, given half a chance, not to mention the fact that they cause great waves to slosh about, upsetting every other craft on the river, and scare the living daylights out of any bird within half a mile of the banks. No, you'll never see me in a motorboat.'

'You stand convicted as a landlubber,' Vincent drawled, winking at her. 'You had better give Sean one of your seductive looks if you want to retrieve your reputation.'

The other two roared with laughter as Belinda went pink. 'One of my seductive looks?' She lowered her lashes and then glanced at him through them. 'I don't know what you mean!'

'Yes, that's the sort of look I meant!' he mocked, and her pulses went crazy at the way he was smiling at her. It wasn't fair; he had more charm than he had any right to, and whenever she tried to be angry with him he disarmed her far too easily.

'Well, let's get this show on the road before you lose the best part of the afternoon!' Sean said, screwing up

his eyes and glancing up at the sun. 'Give me a hand
getting the boat into the water, Vincent. It is a bit of a
performance, even with the slipway so handy.'

It was almost ten minutes before the boat was launched
and Vincent extended a hand to Belinda so that she could
step down into it from the little wooden jetty. She was
faintly nervous because the rowing-boat looked much
smaller on the river and rather ominously rocked to and
fro on the tide, but Vincent's grip was firm and, after
taking a deep breath, she gingerly stepped down, then
sat down almost at once. Sean and Bridie pushed them
off, waving and calling cheerfully as Vincent rowed away.

'Enjoy yourselves! We'll have a cup of tea waiting
when you get back!'

There were quite a few other craft out on the river,
including a number of speedboats whose antics immediately convinced Belinda that Sean was right in his opinion
of motorboats. As they tore past they made the rowing-
boat toss and tumble violently on the water, and she had
to grab hold of the sides of the boat, her body tense with
nerves while she waited for the turbulence to subside.

Vincent swore, his brows black and jagged with rage.
'Damned things! They shouldn't be allowed out on the
river if they won't respect the rights of other river-users.'
Looking at Belinda with concern, he asked, 'Are you
OK? You're not going to be sick, are you?'

'I hope not,' she said.

'So do I!' he murmured feelingly, and she had to smile.
After a few moments, Vincent rowed on along the bank,
under drooping willows which made a green shade for
them, a rustling, whispering tent through which birds
flew and called and sunlight filtered. Vincent rowed with
what even to Belinda's ignorant eyes looked like expert
skill, his slim body bending gracefully, his brown hands

making the oars obey without apparent effort. His strokes were smooth and even; the boat seemed to fly along over the surface of the river.

As she grew more used to the motion of the boat, she leaned over and let one hand trail through the water, delighted by the coolness slipping through her fingers. It was such a hot day, and the feel of the water was refreshing. She took off the white wide-brimmed hat, now that they had moved out of the glare of the after-noon sun, carefully laid it behind her, and turned her face upward to watch the trickle of sunlight through the long, green riband-like willow branches, sliding a hand around her nape under her heavy hair to lift it away from her neck.

'I'm so hot. I think I really must have my hair cut one day next week.'

'Don't you dare!' Vincent exploded, and she looked at him with a sort of shock at the vehemence of that tone, flushing, then looked away hurriedly, her long hair falling back as she let go of it. To hide the unnerving effect of the way he had looked at her, she bent to stare at the river, her hair hanging around her face, drooping like the willows, almost to the water's edge as she leaned over the side.

She saw her own reflection in the glassy surface of the river: drowsy, disturbed green eyes, full of secrets, sunlit, coppery hair, the pale oval of her face, glimmering like the moon caught in the depths of the water.

Vincent slowed his stroke and the boat softly glided into the bank and bumped it slightly. Belinda looked round in alarm, to see him tie up by looping a rope around an exposed tree root.

'Are we going ashore?' she asked hurriedly, and Vincent shook his head.

'I'm tired of rowing, that's all. I thought I'd stretch out and have a rest before we row back.'

She watched in stupefaction as he lay down full-length, his head pillowed on one of the cushions they had brought from the hotel, and shut his eyes.

'You aren't going to sleep?'

'Just for ten minutes, maybe. It's Sean's fault—that meal was distinctly soporific, especially on a hot summer day like this, and the rowing was the last straw.' He yawned widely, showing even white teeth. Like a shark, she thought grimly. She should call him Jaws. 'I don't know how I've kept my eyes open...' His voice slowed, then died away; he stretched lazily, yawning again, while she stared at him.

After a moment, she realised he was sleeping, his arm crooked above his head, half-shielding his eyes from the light, his face relaxed and smooth. Belinda thought of lying down herself, but the boat wasn't big enough for both of them to stretch out. Vincent's feet were right up in her end of the boat. She rather ruefully studied his footwear—cream shoes, beautifully sewn, and un-doubtedly handmade, from the look of them. She ten-tatively brushed a finger over the leather to find it silky smooth and very pliable. He wore cream socks, too, she noticed, her eyes wandering slowly up the length of his body.

She had never before had a chance to stare at him without being observed. Asleep, Vincent was no threat to her, and yet for some odd reason he was more of a threat than he had ever been before. She felt a strangely intense curiosity. Little things that should be mean-ingless somehow seemed loaded with meaning.

She couldn't explain, for instance, why she was so fas-cinated by the way his shirt clung to his skin. He had taken off his jacket and tie when he began to row; his collar was open and the two top buttons of his shirt were undone, giving her a glimpse of dark hair on his chest, the faintest golden sheen of perspiration on his neck. His long, lean body was totally at ease, his mouth a warm line, his dark lashes almost brushing his sun-flushed cheek. She stared at his face, her mouth dry, and that was when she saw the butterfly.

It was large and vivid, peacock-colours of blue and green, with dark circles of glittering dust on the wings. It flew out from the willows and hovered over Vincent's head for a moment while she watched it, then alighted on his cheek.

Vincent frowned and shifted, his breathing changing; he put up a hand and flicked at his face, but the butterfly didn't fly away, it sat there, opening and closing its wings, antennae curling, as if it tasted the air or Vincent's skin, and found it sweet.

It was very beautiful, but it was waking him up, and suddenly Belinda didn't want that. She felt a surge of protective anxiety. He looked so peaceful that it would be a shame to wake him. She very carefully knelt upright and leaned forward to flap a hand at the butterfly to drive it away, but her movement made the boat rock about. She tried to sit down again, but that only made matters worse, and instead of sitting down she was thrown forward and landed on top of Vincent with a thud.

'What the——?' he grunted as she hit him, her body landing with a force that knocked the breath out of her for a moment.

Vincent was still drugged with sleep. He instinctively grabbed her, his hands powerful, and then his eyes

opened wide and he stared up at her in open-mouthed
disbelief.

'Are you trying to assassinate me, or is this a se-
duction attempt?' he drawled, looking amused, but
Belinda didn't find anything in the situation funny. She
was very pink and breathless, her heart knocking inside
her chest as if it were trying to get out. She was lying
full length on top of Vincent, her breasts pressing against
his chest, her legs somehow entwined with his in the fall.
The intimacy of it was unbearable.

'Neither! Let go. I was just...there was a butterfly,
and I...but the boat rocked about, and then...' She
was stammering, husky and incoherent, and Vincent
listened with a crooked little smile, one brow rising.

'You were trying to catch a butterfly? Do you collect
them?'

'No,' she explained impatiently. 'I wasn't trying to
catch it. I was trying to drive it away. It had settled on
you.'

'Oh! And you thought it might bite me?' he enquired
in bland tones that somehow made her feel even more
stupid.

'I thought it might wake you up!'

'So you threw yourself on top of me to save me? How
brave. Weren't you afraid it might bite you instead?'

She gave him a look of intense dislike. 'Oh, don't be
ridiculous. I'm sorry I fell on you—now, will you please
let me get up?'

'Oh, not yet,' he said softly. 'This is nice.' He ran one
hand along her spine, pressing her closer. 'Very nice.'

Panic rose inside her and she pushed at his shoulders,
wriggling furiously in a desperate attempt to get free.
Vincent lay beneath her, watching her with that mocking
smile, his eyes glinting. She tried not to look at his eyes,

and her own gaze fell, but that was even more dangerous, because she found herself staring at the hard, male
line of his mouth, a terrible need mounting inside her.
She swallowed, and looked away, increasing her
struggles, but the arm across her back was like an iron
band, even though his hand stroked up and down her
body like the brush of a butterfly. His other hand began
to be busy, too; she felt it become entwined in her hair
and alarm bells went off in her head.

'Don't——' she began, too late, as he forced her head
down. She got one glimpse of his grey eyes before his
mouth captured hers and changed everything. An intense pleasure shot through her and shamefully she felt
herself melt like a dwindling candle, her limbs weak, her
mouth parting eagerly to meet his kiss. She was appalled
by herself; this time it was worse than it had been when
he had kissed her before. She might have told herself
she wanted to get away from him, but the truth was that
while she lay on top of him she had been looking at his
mouth through her lashes and dying for him to kiss her,
hadn't she?

She must be crazy. Was she forgetting all the reasons
she had for hating him? She knew the sort of man
Vincent Garrett was—and why she must not let this
happen. He was taking advantage of her own folly; it
meant nothing to him but a sudden opportunity to snatch
a little enjoyment. He didn't care twopence for her; he
was still capable of hurting her if it suited him.

She began to resist with a fatalistic sense of desperation, fighting to pull her head back, but aware that he
was much stronger and she had no chance against his
strength. At the back of her mind a cold little voice
asked, But do you really want to stop him, anyway?
Belinda didn't know, didn't want to know, but she gave

up her struggle to break away. Her arms went round his
neck, her mouth moved hotly on his, she moulded her
body to the lean hardness of the body underneath her,
and Vincent gave a deep, husky groan, shuddering.

'Oh, yes, Bell, yes...'

It was the most intense physical experience she had
ever had; consumed by sweetness, dying of pleasure, she
lost all sense of everything outside the two of them, her
whole being given over to touching Vincent, kissing him,
feeling his hands touch her. He had unzipped her dress;
one hand ran down her naked back, his cool fingers
brushing her skin, undoing her bra strap before the hand
moved again and found her breasts. Belinda gave a sharp
cry of desire and at that instant the boat rocked violently
as another of the speedboats rocketed past, sending a
great wash of violent water boiling along the banks.

Belinda found herself being thrown sideways. The boat
tipped that way with her and she gave a gasp of fear as
she felt herself tumbling into the water, but Vincent
grabbed hold of her and dragged her back into the boat
before she actually went down into the river. Gasping
and shivering, she sat up. Her hair had got wet; water
streamed down her face, dripping down her dress, too.

'Are you OK?' asked Vincent, his voice still husky
and unsteady.

She nodded, not quite daring to meet his eyes.

'We'd better get back quickly so that you can dry that
wet hair,' he said. 'I don't want you getting pneumonia
just as you're almost back to normal.'

Back to normal? she thought bleakly. How could he
say she was back to normal when she kept acting in a
way she found decidedly abnormal? Every time Vincent
touched her she was swamped by sensual desires she had
never felt before, and simply couldn't understand. If she

had been in love with him she could have understood it—love and desire were faces of the same coin, after all—but she hated Vincent, she didn't love him. She had begun to feel she might possibly like him, actually, but that was as far as it went, a very tentative feeling that was too new for her to be sure of it. It didn't, couldn't, explain the urgency and hunger with which she had melted into his arms just now. And if it wasn't really Vincent himself she wanted, was it what she had feared— a physical side-effect of her brain injury? Was she suffering spells of being crazy?

'God knows what Bridie and Sean are going to say when they see you,' Vincent drawled. 'They're going to think I've forgotten how to row! They'll never let me forget this, bringing you back looking as if you've been in the river!'

She had her head down and was struggling with her bra strap, but the thing evaded her fingers. She knew Vincent was watching her, but she didn't risk looking at him.

'Let me!' he said drily. 'Turn round.'

Very flushed, she obeyed, closing her eyes involuntarily as she again felt his fingers on her bare back. Even in this practical gesture, the brush of his skin on her own had that wild physical intensity; her heart missed a beat and she bitterly upbraided herself. Stop it! she thought. Stop it! He reclipped her bra, then zipped up her dress with deft speed.

'There you are,' he murmured behind her, and a second later she heard him sit down again and pick up the oars, then slide them into place with a grating sound. Belinda sat down, her wet hair still dripping down her back. She stared into the water as the boat began to move.

'Why did you bring me to your own house?' she asked quietly, conscious of the quick dart of his eyes and, although she did not look at him, the busy rush of his equally quick mind. She knew him so much better now; she knew he was thinking up the best answer to give her, and it was unlikely to be the truth. Vincent Garrett was a stranger to the truth.

'I've explained all that. I know my family have caused you a lot of pain, and I wanted to be sure you were getting the best possible care.'

She laughed bitterly. 'Oh, you're admitting Ricky's responsibility now, are you?'

'Ricky was driving the car, but he was not responsible for the accident. You'll find that I'm not lying, Belinda. The police reports will make that very clear. No, you must know I wasn't just talking about the crash or your physical health.' He sounded very serious, his voice deep. 'Ricky hurt you, I know that, and I'm sorry. He should never have got involved with you in the first place, but he has always been so used to his own way—he was spoilt, being the youngest. When Meg insisted on going off to France for a year to finish her education, he was so furious that he wanted to hurt her back, which was why he chased you and let you think he loved you.'

'If he loves her, why isn't he happy?' she threw back hoarsely, lifting her head then to glare at him.

He stared back, his brows together. 'What?'

'That's something else I overheard today—that woman said it was obvious that Ricky was miserable, his marriage wasn't working out. Why shouldn't it be working out if Ricky loves that girl and she loves him?'

'Forget Ricky,' Vincent said harshly, the lines of his face icy and implacable. 'Whether he's happy or not is nothing to do with you.'

'That's the real reason why you brought me to your home, instead of letting me go to a nursing home, isn't it?' she accused, her green eyes flashing. 'You wanted to make sure I couldn't contact Ricky; you don't want Ricky to see me. You knew that if Ricky rang the hospital and found out that I had recovered consciousness he would try to find me, and you were ready to do anything to stop us meeting again, so you whisked me away from the hospital and brought me to your own home because that was the only place where you could be sure of manipulating events to suit yourself.'

He didn't deny it, he just stared expressionlessly at her, his eyes narrowed to steely slits.

'You have no scruples, do you?' she muttered, aching with shame at the memory of herself in his arms a few moments ago.

He had made love to her to keep her quiet, to distract her from memories of her brother, although no doubt he would have gone on to seduce her if the moment had been opportune. He had wanted her, he hadn't been acting; she didn't doubt the reality of the desire he had felt while they made love, any more than she doubted her own intense passion. His tongue might lie, but his body couldn't. That had been a very real urgency between them. The difference was that she had fought her physical reactions as much as she could; she had not wanted to give in to them, but they had been stronger than her mental control. Vincent, however, had ruthlessly manipulated even his own sensuality; he had allowed himself to make love to her because it suited him. He wasn't being carried away; that icy mind of his was always in control.

She wished she had some of his cool control. Disliking him as she did, why did he have that shattering effect on her? She wished to heaven she knew.

She had been so much in love with Ricky before the accident. An idea dawned suddenly, her eyes widened—could it be that her body still suffered from that arousal although Ricky was no longer there? Their relationship had ended in an instant, and when she woke up again Ricky was gone, but her desire had not ended, it had merely been channelled towards the first man who touched her—towards Vincent.

She stared blankly at Vincent, who stared back, frowning. Slowly, Belinda said, 'Well, I am going to see Ricky. I want to see him right away.'

She had to see Ricky again at once, to find out if her guesswork was wildly off the mark, or whether she was right and the way Vincent made her feel was merely a chemical reaction because her rioting hormones had been cheated of the man she loved.

CHAPTER SEVEN

'THE hell you will!' Vincent said through tight lips. 'Now, you listen to me——'

'I'm never listening to you again. I've listened to you once too often,' Belinda snapped back. 'I've made up my mind, so don't bother to argue. I am going to see Ricky, even if it is only for the last time.'

Fortunately, they were rapidly approaching the little jetty outside Sean and Bridie's hotel, and she could see Bridie waving to them from the garden.

'You aren't wrecking my brother's marriage before it has started!' Vincent said with violence, and she looked at him with distant eyes.

'Don't keep talking about it, because I'm not listening.' She knew that if she let him say anything he would only come up with more lies, some other very plausible story to keep her away from Ricky. The more she thought about it, the more convinced she was that everything he had done since she recovered consciousness had been designed to keep her and Ricky apart.

She waved to Bridie, somehow conjuring up a bright smile. 'There's Bridie. You'd better stop scowling or she'll wonder what on earth has happened, especially when she sees my wet hair.'

Vincent was watching her with glittering eyes; she could feel the rage inside him, and was relieved as the boat bumped into the wooden piles of the jetty and Bridie laughed and came running to help them tie up, her face mischievous.

'Hey! I thought you were a famous oarsman, Vincent. Don't ruin Sean's boat or he'll strangle you. For a minute there I thought you were going to smash into our landing-stage.'

'Sorry,' Vincent mumbled, a faint redness in his face. 'I must be out of practice.'

Bridie gave Belinda a hand on to dry land, then did a comical doubletake, staring at her hair.

'Don't tell me you fell in!' Her eyes danced with amusement. 'What have you two been up to on the river? Or shouldn't I ask?'

'We haven't been up to anything,' Vincent said shortly, stalking away up through the gardens.

'Oops!' Bridie said, staring after him, then gave Belinda a sideways look of laughing enquiry. 'Do I pick up an atmosphere? I've never seen Vincent in a mood like that before.'

'Well, aren't you lucky?' Belinda said rather sourly, then caught Bridie's surprised expression and relented, sighing. 'Sorry, I didn't mean to bite your head off, but I'm rather off Vincent Garrett at the moment.' She pushed back her damp hair, grimacing. 'My hair smells of the river—sorry to be a nuisance, but could I——?'

'Wash your hair? Of course, be my guest.' Bridie showed her upstairs to a pretty lavender bathroom, provided her with a clean towel, shampoo, and a hairdrier, and left her to it. Belinda washed and rinsed her hair then towelled it lightly before blowing it quite dry and restoring it to its usual condition.

She went back to the hotel lounge to find Vincent with Sean and Bridie, having tea and scones at the table looking out on the river. It was distinctly nerve-racking to walk across the room towards them with Vincent's menacing eyes on her all the way, but she stiffened her spine and held her head up, and made it without a blink.

'You look gorgeous again, damn you!' Bridie said, grinning in a friendly way.

'Thank you,' Belinda said, smiling back, very aware of Vincent but refusing to look in his direction.

'Have some home-made scones. Sean's very proud of them—made with sour milk, the Irish way,' said Bridie. 'Light as a feather, aren't they, Vincent?'

Vincent made a grunting noise that might have meant anything. Belinda was determined to be more gracious than that, so she smiled warmly at Sean and Bridie and said she was very tempted, she did love scones, but really she had eaten far too much that day already. She had a cup of tea, however, but had barely drunk half of it before Vincent suddenly got up and said impatiently that they must be going.

'We've been out for hours and Belinda should be resting; she has only just recovered from a bad accident, after all.'

'Come back and see us again soon,' said Sean and Bridie as they waved them off outside the hotel.

Her white hat firmly anchored on her head, Belinda nodded and waved back. Vincent didn't say anything, but he gave his friends a nod and waved once as they turned the corner to vanish from sight.

Belinda was expecting him to attack her at once, to start another furious argument about her decision to see Ricky, but to her astonishment he didn't say a word. Completely silent, his face in profile to her, his jawline taut, his mouth brooding, and his eyes fixed on the road, he drove like the wind, at a speed that made her very tense.

It was unnerving, and she almost wished he would explode at her, shout, bully her—anything rather than this terrible silence. The trouble was, she didn't know what the silence meant, or what was going on inside his head; and not knowing was even more disturbing because Vincent was capable of anything. So what was he planning exactly? She wished she knew.

They were almost back at his house when she suddenly realised that he had taken a different road, and that they would be passing his parents' house. She sat up straight, staring, wondering if she was mistaken, but no, she saw it a moment later as they took a bend in the road. Big and white, it shimmered like a mirage in the late afternoon sunlight among a cluster of lime-trees and oak trees.

She looked round at Vincent, her green eyes wide and uncertain. 'That's your family home!'

'I did recognise it,' he said tersely without giving her so much as a glance.

'What are we doing here?'

'You said you wanted to see my brother.' The car was slowing down; she couldn't believe it as he spun the wheel and turned in through the gates of the house. Why had he brought her here? Why was he making it possible for her to see his brother after he had gone to so much trouble to keep them apart?

Her dazed eyes flashed over the splendour of the house; it still overawed her, just as the thought of meeting Vincent's parents did.

The gardens were very beautiful, too—formal gardens, with roses and lavender growing between neat, geometric designs made by box hedges, with mossy classical statues at the centre of elaborate patterns bisected by grassy gravel paths. It was an English garden in the traditional mould, set among an acre of smoothly mown lawns, and this afternoon there were people apparently everywhere.

'A croquet party,' Vincent said drily. 'Do you play?'

'No . . . yes . . .'

'Very coherent,' he said, as he braked and parked on the drive in front of the house. He came round and opened her door, viewing her with sardonic coldness. 'Well, do you want to see my brother or don't you?'

Bewildered and utterly thrown off balance, she got out of the car. 'I can't talk to him in front of a crowd of people!' she protested, and was given a look that perturbed her.

'That's the only way you are going to see him,' Vincent grimly told her. 'Let me remind you yet again—he is married. I only brought you here because I hope that if you actually set eyes on him again you'll stop being so obsessed with him. Frankly, I can't understand what you ever saw in him, anyway; he's quite boring, you know, even if he is an attractive enough male animal.'

He took her arm in a firm, compelling grip and headed for the party on the croquet lawn, and Belinda was too stunned to argue or try to break free. Vincent had surprised her yet again; he was always doing that to her, making her rock back on her heels by doing something unexpected. Being around Vincent Garrett was rather like living with a jack-in-the-box which leapt out at you when you were off-guard.

The players in their light summer clothes, some of the men in white, the girls in flimsy, fluttering dresses, strolling elegantly and idly about with their mallets, glanced round towards the new arrivals.

Belinda heard someone say, 'It's Vincent!'

Someone else said, 'But who's that?'

Her nervous eyes flashed around the faces, recognised those of his parents, saw their alarm and disbelief. Then she saw Ricky.

He was turning slowly, smiling, but the smile vanished as he looked at her and recognised her.

He turned pale, eyes rounding, the whites showing as they did on a frightened animal. He dropped the mallet he had been holding. Belinda had a feeling he was going to faint; he visibly swayed. Seeing her was clearly a deep shock to him, and, although she was prepared, it was still an equal shock to her to see Ricky. She went cold, her heart beat slowly and heavily, her sight clouded.

She stopped in her tracks and stared at him, and Ricky just stood there, his eyes eating her up, then he began to run towards her. She shook free of Vincent and began to run too, half laughing, half crying, her hands held out towards Ricky.

She felt Vincent make a movement, as if to pull her back, but he was too late, she was out of his reach.

'Bell!' Ricky called out before he reached her. 'Oh, Bell, is it really you?'

Then he was there, in front of her, his hands out, touching her face, her hair, holding her shoulders while he stared and stared. 'I thought I was seeing things,' he said shakily. 'I thought I'd gone mad. I've been so guilty about you, I couldn't be happy knowing that you...and here you are, looking so——' He broke off, laughing, his eyes wet, his blond hair tumbling down over his forehead. He put a hand to his face, pushed the lock of hair back, rubbed his eyes, gave a choked, embarrassed little laugh. 'Sorry, I'm being stupid, but you can't know how I feel. To see you like this... when I didn't think I ever would again, that you were lost forever, because of me... Oh, Bell, it's a miracle!'

'You didn't know?' she asked slowly, although she was certain now that he had not been told, and Ricky shook his head, still very pale.

'Know? Of course not, I'd no idea...when did it happen? I mean, how long have you been... I can't get over how well you look, as if nothing had ever happened!'

'I recovered consciousness weeks ago,' she said.

'Weeks ago?' he repeated, looking shaken. 'What do you mean, weeks ago? How long ago?'

Quietly she told him the date, and Ricky gave a start, looking very odd, the last vestige of colour ebbing away.

'But that was...'

'Was what?' she asked, and Ricky looked past her slowly, staring at his brother, who was standing just behind them.

'Did you know she had come out of her coma?'

'It was me who brought her here today, wasn't it?' Vincent returned in a level voice.

Ricky's jaw tightened and his eyes had darkness in them. 'You know what I meant—did you know on the day she came out of the coma, or were you told later?'

'If I had known,' Vincent said coolly, 'what on earth would have been the point of telling you and spoiling that day for you and Meg?'

Belinda had been puzzled for a moment, but suddenly she knew; oh, she knew what had made Ricky go white and look so shaken.

She found it hard to breathe for a second as it hit her. She had come out of the coma on Ricky's wedding day! Vincent had lied to her about that, too. She hadn't recovered consciousness a week later; it had happened on the very day of the wedding, and Vincent had been told. He had known and he had kept the news to himself to make quite sure that the marriage went ahead as planned. He had been afraid, no doubt, that if Ricky knew he would not go through with his wedding.

Vincent was watching her as she looked at him; his face was unreadable, but she hoped he could read the icy contempt she felt for him.

'How could you do that? I ought to kill you!' Ricky's face broke up into violence as he dived towards Vincent, snarling, but his brother grabbed his wrists and pulled his arms downwards, staring past him, over his shoulder. 'Meg is coming. Pull yourself together!'

The whiplash of his tone made Ricky freeze. Vincent let go of him and he stumbled back, confusion in his face.

'I'll never forgive you for this!' he muttered to his brother. 'You had no right to keep it from me!'

Belinda wished she hadn't come here, she was in no condition to face the woman who had taken Ricky away from her—but she couldn't run away, so she gritted her teeth and turned to confront Ricky's wife, not sure what to expect, but ready to hate her.

Meg was not what she had been expecting. The glamorous, spoilt rich girl of her imagination had been a very different creature from this tiny, delicately built girl, with a great deal of soft browny gold hair and shy blue eyes. She was not what you could call beautiful—her features were quite ordinary and her figure was slight—but she had a sweetness of expression that was uncounterfeited, a smile that held warmth and gentleness. Belinda had hoped to hate her, but she couldn't.

'Hello, Vincent!' she said as she joined them. 'I'm so glad you could come, after all. It seems ages since we saw you, doesn't it, Ricky, darling?' But her eyes kept darting at Belinda, curiosity in her face.

'Ages,' Ricky mumbled, eyes on the ground.

His wife gave Vincent a kiss on the cheek, standing on tiptoe to do it because he was a head taller than herself. 'And you've brought someone with you—that's nice,' she said, holding out a hand to Belinda. 'Hello. I'm Meg Garrett, Ricky's wife. We haven't met, have we?'

Belinda slowly held out her own hand, wondering if the other girl knew about her. Would her name make Ricky's wife turn pale? Clearly, Meg had noticed Ricky's emotion on seeing her. Before she gave her name, though, Vincent beat her to it, his voice calm.

'This is Belinda Hunt, Meg. You haven't met her before, but you'll be seeing a lot of her in future because we just got engaged.'

Belinda's eyes dilated in shock. What had he said? She looked up at him and Vincent's cold eyes ordered her not to say a word. She would have ignored him, but she was so shattered that for the moment she was dumb.

Ricky was equally stunned; he stared from her to Vincent and back again, opened his mouth, closed it, swallowed visibly. Obviously he was about to burst out with an incredulous question, but Meg spoke first.

Of the three of them, she looked the least amazed. She was startled, clearly, but her face had brightened, the curiosity had gone. 'Oh, you two are engaged! So that's why Ricky looked so excited! He didn't tell me this was in the wind! Ricky, you might have said something! After all, I'm one of the family now. But it's wonderful news! I'm very happy for both of you.'

'Thank you,' said Vincent blandly, sliding an arm around Belinda's waist in a possessive gesture. She would have resisted, but she was still dazed and just stared up at him in what to an outsider might have looked like dreamy bliss. In fact, it was mere stupefaction.

Ricky had finally managed to get a word out. 'You're really getting married?' he said hoarsely, and Meg looked at him, laughing.

'I know how you feel, darling. Do you know, it's very odd—my father said only the other day that one marriage always leads to a string of others. It puts ideas into people's heads. He'll be amused to hear his prophecy come true this quickly. I'm quite sure he didn't think it would be Vincent who proved him right!' She gave her brother-in-law a teasing, affectionate look. 'Sorry, Vin, dear, but you do have a reputation for being the toughest old bachelor around. I don't suppose Dad would have predicted you for the matrimonial stakes! By the way, are you announcing it? Is it something we can talk about? Or do you want to keep it quiet for a bit?'

'We don't want it made public for a while, no,' Vincent said slowly. 'We'll keep it in the family, I think, for a few days.' His eyes darted towards the other guests and a little frown crossed his face.

Meg's gaze followed his and she grimaced. 'Of course, I understand—you'll have to break it to——' She broke off, giving Belinda a quick look, going rather pink. 'To your parents,' she hurriedly and rather unconvincingly added.

Belinda was just beginning to think again after the first shock of incredulity. She realised why Vincent had invented that ridiculous lie—he wanted to distract Meg from any suspicions she might otherwise have had about Ricky. His obvious emotion at the sight of her would have needed some explanation, and on the spur of the moment Vincent had come up with this engagement. Clever of him! Not only did it explain why Ricky was so excited, but it had completely distracted Meg from any close examination of her husband's face, and given her other ideas to think about.

Belinda looked up at Vincent herself, angry irony in her eyes. Ah, but what if she decided to blow his lie sky-high? What if she told Meg the truth?

He glanced down, aware of her scrutiny, and stared at her, those cold grey eyes probing her expression, his mouth indenting with impatience as he read the thoughts she did not hide.

'Are you two going to finish this game or not?' a new voice called at that instant, and they all looked round.

'Oh, dear,' murmured Meg, throwing Vincent a half-laughing look. 'Does Magdalen know about Belinda?'

Belinda stiffened, recognising the name first, and then, with a long stare, the face of the girl sauntering towards them, a croquet mallet over her shoulder as if she were a soldier on guard duty. Magdalen was the girl in the photograph which she had dropped—the girl whose sleek black hair and sensual, faintly sullen pout she remembered so well. She was even lovelier than her photograph, or perhaps that was the effect of sunlight and the figure-flattering white dress she wore.

'We'll distract her!' Meg said, grabbing Ricky's hand and pulling him towards the other girl. 'Just coming, Magdalen!' Ricky went, but looked back at Belinda with eyes which still seemed dazed with shock. She watched him go in a quiet sadness that was like the ebb of some slow, irreversible tide. She had not said goodbye to him until now; she had not really believed he was married, that it was over between them, but now that she had seen him with Meg she finally accepted it, and let go, not with grief or pain, but at most a faint melancholy.

Magdalen had almost reached them when Meg and
Ricky met her. Meg linked arms with her, talking a blue
streak. Magdalen was staring at Vincent and Belinda,
and seemed determined to join them, but Meg pulled
her away, back towards the other guests.

'She's a wonderful girl,' Vincent suddenly said.

'Who, your girlfriend?' Belinda coldly mocked him.
'I'm sure she is, but let's hope she's very understanding.
If she hears about this "engagement" she isn't going to
be too happy, is she? That will teach you to tell lies
without thinking twice about it.'

'I meant Meg,' he said tersely. 'She will make Ricky
happy, Bell; admit it now. You've seen them together—
they were meant for each other, you can't deny that.'

She wasn't even going to try. Obviously, Vincent hadn't
lied about one thing—Ricky had turned to her out of
pique and resentment because Meg had not given in to
him and got married instead of finishing her education.
Having seen them together, Belinda believed he loved
Meg and would be happy with her; not that she had any
intention of admitting as much to Vincent.

Ricky's deeply emotional reaction to the sight of her
had been fuelled by guilt, not love. He had been driving
when the car crashed; he had seen her lying there for
months as if dead. He must have been overwhelmed by
a terrible burden of guilt, especially knowing that he
wanted to marry someone else and had never really loved
her the way he did Meg. She knew now why Ricky had
not looked the picture of radiant happiness since his
wedding. Poor Ricky, how could he allow himself to be
happy with Meg when he felt responsible for what had
happened to her?

'You've seen them,' Vincent repeated, watching her with a frown on his face. 'They are meant for each other!'

'And you and Magdalen—were you meant for each other?' she asked instead, smiling maliciously at him. 'What are you going to tell her, by the way? Got your excuses ready? I hope they're very plausible. She doesn't look as if she is as naïve as I am. In fact, she looks even tougher and more ruthless than you are, and I hope she tears you limb from limb. I can't wait to watch you get what you so richly deserve.'

She broke free from him and walked away, not back towards the car, but following the other three to the croquet lawn. After a moment of stunned immobility, Vincent came after her, almost running, but he was too late to stop her catching up with Meg, Ricky and Magdalen.

'I haven't played croquet for years,' she said brightly, joining them. 'I can't remember the rules!'

'I'll be happy to teach you,' said Meg, but Belinda smiled back, shaking her head, then fluttered her lashes up at Vincent as he arrived beside them, a grim expression in his grey eyes.

'Thank you, Meg, but Vincent will teach me how to play, won't you, darling?' she purred seductively, putting one finger on his arm and running it lightly and flirtatiously up to his shoulder.

'Some other time, I think!' he said through his teeth, grabbing hold of her wrist and trying to drag her away. She resisted, laughing gaily.

'Isn't he masterful?' she asked Magdalen, who was watching with sharp, hostile eyes. 'Now, don't be mean, Vincent darling. I want to meet Meg's friend. Hello— I'm Belinda, Vincent's fiancée. How do you do?' She

held out a hand to Magdalen, who considered it like
someone eyeing a snake.

'Fiancée?' Magdalen repeated in a shrill voice, an ugly
look on her face. From a distance she was far more
beautiful than she was at close quarters, when you saw
the sullen pout of her mouth and the hardness of her
brown eyes.

'Yes, we've just got engaged today!' Belinda said,
leaning on Vincent, her head against his shoulder. She
felt the angry tension in his body, and knew he would
make her pay for what she was doing, but she didn't
care. She was getting her own back for all the pain and
heartache he had put her through.

Magdalen tore her eyes away from Belinda and looked
at Vincent. A slow, dark flush filled her face, and her
eyes spat rage. She didn't say anything, and Vincent said
nothing, either. He just stared back, his face quite blank.
Belinda had half expected him to deny it, laugh and say
it was just a joke, or something. Anything. The silence
was awful, and Belinda began to wish she hadn't given
in to her impulse to take such a petty revenge. She
shouldn't have lost her temper.

Then, throwing down her croquet mallet in a violent
gesture, Magdalen suddenly walked off without a
backward glance.

'Oh, goodness!' Meg said, biting her lip. 'Should I go
after her, do you think? She's so upset.'

'She's so livid!' Ricky said, grimacing. 'She wanted
Vin herself. An ambitious lady, our Magdalen. She'll get
over it, Meg, don't worry.'

Meg shook her head at him, her gentle face reproachful. 'That's not kind, Ricky. Poor girl. I think
I'd better go and see if I can help.'

She hurried away and Ricky watched her go, smiling crookedly. 'Meg is always so damn soft-hearted. Who else would think of Magdalen as a poor girl?'

'You'd better go with her,' Vincent said, his eyes grimly set on Belinda, and his brother gave him a furious look, scowling.

'Don't order me around! I'm not taking any more orders from you, Vincent! Don't think I've forgotten or forgiven that you kept it from me that Belinda was better. You knew I was out of my mind with worry——'

'Not enough to make you visit her at the hospital, however,' Vincent said coldly. 'Or you would have found out she had recovered.'

Ricky went red. 'You made me promise I'd never go there again! You swore you would take care of everything.'

'Oh, did he?' bit out Belinda. So that was why Ricky had made no enquiries about her. Vincent had made him promise to stay away! 'He certainly took care of me!' she told Ricky angrily. 'He kidnapped me——'

'Kidnapped you?' Ricky looked horrified, incredulous. 'You can't be serious.'

'Oh, yes, I am! He forced me to live in his house——'

'In his house?' Ricky's jaw dropped and he stared at his brother. 'You've had her in your house?'

Vincent didn't get a chance to answer because Belinda was still reciting her charges against him, her voice feverish. 'He lied and schemed, and even descended to——' She broke off, very flushed, and Ricky stared at her, lifting his eyebrows.

'Yes, descended to what?'

Vincent said coldly, 'We agreed that Belinda was my problem in future, not yours, Ricky. Why don't you just go and find your wife?'

Belinda stiffened, a little trickle of ice running down her spine. So, she was a 'problem' he had taken on, was she? Vincent Garrett was such a busy man, always fixing something, manoeuvring or manipulating someone. Well, he had just manoeuvred himself into trouble, and she meant to see that he got it.

Ricky gave his brother a mischievous look. 'I'll go after Meg in a moment, Vin. First, I want to know exactly what you descended to! Bell looks so agitated that it has to be fascinating.'

'Oh, it is!' Belinda said viciously. 'I can tell you a few things about your brother. He is an unscrupulous, ruthless, lying...' She couldn't get another word out, she was too angry. She looked back over the last few days and was literally choked with fury.

'But I thought you two were engaged,' Ricky said, frowning.

'We are,' Vincent said curtly. 'Ricky, I want a word alone with you...' He drew him aside, lowering his voice so that Belinda couldn't hear. What was he saying about her? she wondered crossly, and edged closer in time to hear Vincent say, 'Can't you see she isn't quite over the effects of the accident? We have to treat her with kid gloves. For the moment, she's prone to bursts of violent temper, and gets confused——'

'You liar!' roared Belinda, and they both looked round at her, startled by the sheer volume of her voice.

Ricky looked shaken, and Vincent said with a sigh, 'You see what I mean? Now, Ricky, don't ask her any more questions. She mustn't get overexcited, or who knows what might happen? The mind is a delicate in-

strument—even the doctors don't seem quite sure what
to expect in her case.'

'I heard that! I heard that!' Belinda erupted, almost
dancing with fury.

'Now, Belinda! Don't upset yourself,' soothed
Vincent, and she glared at him, her green eyes flashing.

'Stop hinting that I'm crazy! There's nothing wrong
with my mind, and I won't have you saying there is!
Don't think I don't know what you're up to. Every time
I turn around you're up to something. Utterly ruthless,
that's what you are. You turn everything to your own
advantage, don't you? Unscrupulous, devious...no,
devious is too polite. Call a spade a spade! You're not
just devious. You're a liar. Well, it serves you right that
I took a leaf out of your book...it was your idea in the
first place...now you see what happens when chickens
come home to roost!'

Ricky looked very unhappy at this deluge of words;
he began backing away hastily. 'Sorry, Vin, you're right,'
he told his brother in a low voice. 'Stupid of me, but
she looks so normal. Is she going to be OK in the end,
though? I mean——'

'I am perfectly normal!' Belinda snapped, shaking
with temper.

'Of course you are,' Vincent soothed, putting an arm
round her.

She shot out of reach, looking at him with hatred.
'Don't you touch me! I don't want you anywhere near
me!'

'Should she have left hospital?' Ricky asked, his
expression appalled.

'I think all this is just because it is her first day out,'
Vincent said. 'She'll be fine, once she's safely back in
her room. She needs peace and quiet for a few days, and

I think it would be better if she doesn't see you again for quite a while, Ricky. I realise you're concerned, naturally you are, and it does you credit, but you're married now, and your first loyalty is to Meg, and, anyway, you can't do Belinda any good. Sorry to be so brutal, but the best thing you can do for her is to stay away.'

'I feel so terrible about this,' Ricky said, biting his lip, then began to back away, eyeing Belinda with uneasy sympathy. 'I'm sorry, Bell—about the accident, I mean. It wasn't my fault, I hope you realise that. The lorry just came out of nowhere and I couldn't avoid it, but even so I feel guilty. I wish there were something I could do to make all this up to you. It's been such a dreadful time for you, I know that. Anything I can do for you, just ask, remember. Anything at all.'

He looked just like an anxious little boy all at sea as to what he should do. Poor Ricky. She smiled reassuringly at him. 'Don't worry, I'm fine, ignore what your brother said. I'm going to be OK, really!'

That seemed to make him feel worse; he smiled shakily. 'Oh, Bell, you're wonderful,' he said, and then he fled.

Belinda turned on Vincent once Ricky was out of earshot. 'Well, I hope you're satisfied with yourself!' she shouted. 'The nerve of it! Telling him I'm off my head! I'd been asking myself what more you could do to me. You've taken everything else away from me— what else could you do? I wondered. Now I know! You can make everyone think I'm crazy and not responsible for what I say or do. Well, I'm not going to let you get away with it. You can tell Ricky the truth. Do you hear me? You know you were lying. You know perfectly well that I know exactly what I'm saying and doing!'

He listened until she came to a breathless halt, then said, his grey eyes gleaming with mockery, 'Of course I know you're perfectly sane, and I'm delighted you know what you're saying, because you just told the world that we were getting married—and you're going to have to go through with it.'

CHAPTER EIGHT

FOR a long, long moment Belinda just stared at Vincent, dumbfounded, then she said scornfully, 'That isn't funny.'

'It wasn't meant to be,' he said, in a casual manner, his gaze wandering away from her towards the croquet party. His face changed. 'And now that you've seen my brother, we'll be on our way,' he said abruptly.

Belinda's eyes had automatically followed his and seen what he saw: his parents heading towards them with set, angry faces.

She started to laugh. 'Now you're for it! Your mother and father look as if they're ready to kill you.' She did not disguise the fact that she would queue to watch them do it, too.

Vincent gave her a hard stare, then fastened his long fingers around her wrist and began to stride away, dragging her reluctantly after him.

'Not so fast! I'm tired,' she protested, and he at once slowed, giving her a searching look.

'Yes, you do look tired. Damn! I shouldn't have brought you here. It was too much for you at the end of your first day out!'

Belinda laughed suddenly, forced to be honest for some reason. He had driven her crazy, he was devious and ruthless, but she felt a surge of gratitude because she had been locked away from the world for so long, and today, for the first time in many months, she had felt really alive, thanks to him.

'Oh, but I had such fun!' she said, her green eyes bright, her smile a little tremulous. 'Thank you for my day out.'

He stared down at her oddly, his own smile crooked. 'Not at all. I enjoyed it, too.' There was a brief pause as they stared at each other, then detaching his eyes from her face in a slow way, he looked over her shoulder and groaned.

'My parents don't give up, do they? Look, get in the car—I won't be a minute.'

He put her into the passenger seat of the car and walked away to meet Mr and Mrs Garrett.

His father had greying hair now, but it had once been Vincent's colour, and there were other resemblances, too, in height and features. You could see at a glance that they were father and son; the likeness was quite striking. His mother was more like Ricky; she had silvery fair hair and blue eyes and was fine-boned. In the family photographs which Belinda had seen in Vincent's house they had been smiling, but they were not looking very happy now.

Belinda watched from a distance, wondering what they were saying to Vincent. Something very angry, from their expressions! Of course, it served him right, announcing without warning that they were engaged simply to stop Ricky's wife from asking any awkward questions. Belinda had been furious with him, and then Magdalen had come along and she had acted on impulse, in a temper, and for the sheer hell of it.

She had wanted to annoy Vincent, for one thing; for another she had wanted her revenge for all the things he had said and done to her ever since they met. There was another reason—if she was honest! She had disliked Magdalen instantly, from seeing her photograph, even

before they met. For no particular reason; it was nothing
to do with Vincent—she just didn't like Magdalen's face.

Vincent suddenly spun on his heel and strode back
towards the car, scowling. Belinda considered his
expression ruefully. Oh, dear, she thought. Now he really
is in a temper.

He opened his car door, slid inside, slammed the door
shut, started the engine and drove away—all without
looking at her or uttering as much as a syllable. Belinda
sat very still in her seat, viewing him sideways through
lowered lashes, deciding that it would be much wiser to
hold her tongue for the moment. Vincent was quite formidable at most times, but when he looked like that he
really rather scared her. She could imagine what effect
he had on his business opponents. No wonder he was
so successful.

They arrived back at Dillingham Place without
speaking, and while he was putting the car away Belinda
hurried into the house with a sigh of relief at having
escaped from his brooding presence. She had had the
feeling that any minute now he might explode into wrath.

Jess met her in the hall and looked scoldingly at her.
'So you're back at last! I was beginning to get really
worried. You've been gone for hours! I'm surprised at
Vincent, keeping you out all this time. He should know
better than that. You're still supposed to be going carefully. This is a convalescent period, remember. You can't
just racket about all over the country as you like. I
suppose you didn't have your rest in the middle of the
afternoon?'

Belinda shook her head, giving Jess a coaxing, apolo-
getic smile. 'I'm sorry if you were worried, but I'm fine,
really. We had a wonderful time, had the most delicious

lunch, then went on the river in a rowing-boat——'

'I hope you didn't do any of the rowing!'

'No, Vincent did all the work.'

'Well, up to bed at once. I think you should have a very light supper in bed tonight and get some good rest. I'll bring your meal up on a tray in half an hour.' Jess shooed her up the stairs with a wave of her hands and Belinda did not argue; she was quite happy to obey, especially as it would mean escaping from Vincent and any repercussions from the events at his family home.

She got undressed, had a bath and got into bed some fifteen minutes later. She heard the telephone ring as she picked up the book she had been reading last night. Magdalen? she wondered, her mouth twisting.

Well, even if it were—was it her business? Why should she care if a dozen women rang Vincent Garrett? He was nothing to her. She stared at a page, all the little black words blurring before her eyes. This really was a very boring book. Why was she wasting her time on it?

The door opened and she sat upright, staring fixedly at the page.

'Here you are,' said Jess, coming across the room, and Belinda's heart unaccountably sank.

'Oh, thank you,' she mumbled, pushing her book aside and allowing Jess to set the tray down across her knees.

'I just made you some toast and scrambled eggs,' Jess said, neglecting to mention the snippets of smoked salmon she had whisked into the egg. 'And then strawberries and cream.'

'Gorgeous!' Belinda said, rather wanly picking up her fork. She tasted the eggs while Jess watched, and knew she had to display enthusiasm or hurt Jess's feelings. 'Mmm. They melt in the mouth!' she said.

Jess looked satisfied, and turned to go. 'I'll be back for the tray and to turn out your light in a little while.'

'I'm not five years old!' Belinda protested.

'You just act like it?'

Belinda pretended to be amused, which wasn't easy. Smiling, Jess went and Belinda ate her meal without any real appetite, then put the tray down on the floor and settled back in bed. Who had she been expecting when Jess arrived? she irritably asked herself. Not Vincent. She didn't want to see Vincent, and yet she had felt her heart miss a beat when the door opened, felt stupid disappointment as she saw it was Jess.

Surely she wasn't beginning to——? She shut off that thought, horrified. No! She wasn't in any way attracted to Vincent Garrett; she disliked him intensely. It was just that emotions were confusing; it was sometimes hard to disentangle the threads of them, buried deep inside yourself.

Strange how little she now felt about Ricky, for instance. Ever since she had recovered consciousness she had believed she was aching to see him again. She had woken up that first day as deeply in love as she had been on the day of the crash, and she wasn't quite sure when her feelings had changed. Certainly not when Vincent had told her Ricky had abandoned her and married Meg. A little frown creased her forehead as she remembered what Ricky had blurted out. She had recovered consciousness on the day he married Meg! Wasn't that strange? It couldn't be a coincidence, surely? How had she known, though? Had she heard people talking, even though she was unconscious? How else could she have picked up the fact that Ricky was marrying someone else? The nurses must have gossiped about the wedding, it would only have been natural. It was odd, though.

Well, however it had happened, it had brought about the miracle she needed—it had brought her back to life.

She had been bitterly unhappy when Vincent had told her about the wedding and for a long time after that—yet now it no longer mattered. The change in her feelings had been subterranean and very gradual, but she faced the fact now. She no longer loved Ricky.

She didn't blame him for what had happened, either. Ricky hadn't caused the crash; he had been weak, he had run out on her when she needed him, but he couldn't help his own nature, and she could see now that she would never have been happy with him. Her love for him had been an illusion. Now that she saw him more clearly she felt an affectionate tolerance for him. Now that she no longer loved Ricky she could like him.

She liked Meg, too. She had liked her on sight just as she had disliked Magdalen that fast. She grimaced ruefully, recognising her own instant reactions as a dangerous risk. Wasn't that how she had convinced herself she was madly in love with Ricky? One look and she was telling herself she was in love. How stupid could you get?

A wry smile lit her face, as she remembered Ricky's expression when he had first seen her coming towards him. He had been so shaken. For a second she had been overcome to see him; for a second her emotions had been unbearable, and she could understand how he had felt, because she had been expecting to see him. Ricky hadn't expected to see her and his shock had been visible. But it hadn't been love in his face. Ricky had felt relief and delight, because she had recovered, mingled with shame and guilt over his own behaviour; a complex cocktail of emotions for someone like Ricky, who liked his life smooth and easy.

Belinda yawned. Seeing Ricky had completed the process of recovery in some way. She was certain now that she no longer loved him, she felt free of him, of the past. Her last conscious thought was that tomorrow was Monday; and tomorrow she would ring her mother and then book her flight to New Zealand.

When she got up the next day she found that Vincent had gone to London, to his office. Jess kept her busy that morning, with massage and exercise. Belinda's muscles still ached from the exertions of her Sunday out, so after a light lunch Jess sent her up to bed to have an hour's rest. When she got up again, they walked around the garden, talking.

'You've known Vincent for a long time?' Belinda asked casually, and Jess laughed.

'Oh, all his life. I was at school with his mother, and when she got married I was one of her bridesmaids. We're still friends. She often calls to see me.'

'Then you must have known all about me before I came here?' Belinda looked directly at her and Jess smiled, her face unworried.

'Of course. Dorothy often confides her problems to me.'

'And I was one of them?' grimaced Belinda, and Jess laughed, then, looking at her affectionately.

'I'm afraid so. She was very angry with you. If we're going to be honest, I'd better admit that I didn't like what I'd heard about you, either.'

Belinda couldn't help laughing too, at the cheerful way Jess said that, although at the same time she was hurt. Jess took her hand and squeezed it.

'But I hadn't met you, then. I knew Meg, I've known her for a long time and I'm very fond of her. Both Dorothy and I were certain Meg was the right girl for

Ricky, and we thought you had stolen him. We thought
you had to be a scheming, ambitious gold-digger.' Jess
squeezed her hand again, swinging it between them as
they walked. 'Remember, I hadn't met you then!'

'And now you have, and you know you were right!'
mocked Belinda, to cover her hurt feelings.

'Now I have and I know I was wrong—and I'm very
sorry you've had such a rough time,' Jess said gently,
and Belinda fell silent, touched.

'I think you've walked far enough today, after all that
racketing around you did yesterday!' Jess said a moment
later. 'Time for tea, I think.'

They turned back towards the house just as Vincent's
car swung through the gates and drove towards them.
Jess halted, waving, and he pulled up a few feet away,
got out of the car and joined them, giving Belinda a
quick, all-seeing glance that read her cold expression and
taut body.

'Enjoying yourselves, I see,' he drawled.

'We've had a walk and now we're just going to have
tea. Shall I bring a cup for you, Vincent?' Jess opened
the front door and made for the kitchen, pausing to look
back over her shoulder as he answered.

'Please, I'm dying for some tea.'

Belinda walked into the sitting-room and sat down,
her eyes fixed on the window through which she could
see the garden she had just left.

Vincent followed her and sat down in another chair,
unbuttoning the jacket of his dark grey city suit and
crossing his long legs, his body relaxing into a casual,
lounging attitude. She felt him observing her, but ignored him, watching the way the trees in the garden blew
softly in a summer breeze. There were a few clouds in
the blue sky, too. Maybe the weather was changing?

'My parents are coming to dinner tomorrow night,' he murmured, and she looked at him then, her green eyes wide and startled.

'What?'

'I thought it was high time they got to know you.'

'What are you talking about?' she said impatiently. 'They know me already, and they hate me——'

'They'll have to change their minds after we're married,' Vincent said coolly, and she stiffened, her face hot and angry.

'I didn't think that joke was funny the first time you made it!'

'I told you, it isn't a joke.'

She jumped up, trembling and flushed. 'I'm not listening to any more!' She made for the door, but he barred her way.

'You've got to marry me!' he said tersely.

She stared incredulously into his face and saw he meant that; he wasn't smiling, he was staring back at her, an obduracy in his face that disturbed her.

'I don't know what's behind this——' she began defiantly, and he interrupted her, his mouth crisply biting out his words.

'Common sense, Belinda. If you do bring a law suit against my brother to claim damages for that accident, it could cost my family a fortune. I doubt, personally, if you would win—as I've told you, the accident was not Ricky's fault. However, there is one fact that you're unaware of—Ricky had let his insurance lapse——'

'Oh, the idiot!' she muttered, but was not surprised to hear it because it was just the sort of thing Ricky would do.

Vincent's mouth twisted. 'Yes. Typical, of course; he's always been forgetful. The police know, naturally; he's been charged with driving without insurance, and a couple of other minor charges, but the case hasn't come to court yet. It will be dealt with at the same time as the accident itself. As Ricky didn't cause the accident, he'll probably just be fined, but if it gets out that you mean to bring a case, however, it could do him and the family a lot of damage. After all, you were his passenger. It will look as though you believe Ricky caused the accident, and it could make the police suspicious.'

'I don't remember anything about the accident. I told the police as much when they came to see me in hospital. The whole thing is just a blank. If you're hoping to persuade me to give up my claim, forget it!' she protested. 'I lost eight months of my life, I lost my home and my job, not to mention Ricky himself——'

His eyes hardened. 'We won't go into all that again, thanks! I know the catalogue by heart, you've reeled it off to me often enough. I accept that you have a claim, and I'm offering compensation for all the things you've lost. Marry me, and you get a home and a job combined. I can't give you back the eight months of your life——'

'Or Ricky?' she interrupted drily, but he ignored her.

'But I can give you a good deal, materially speaking. I'm a wealthy man and as my wife you would lead a very comfortable life in future.'

She felt cold; he spoke so offhandedly, his grey eyes remote. It seemed to make a mockery of what they were talking about. Was that what marriage meant to him? What about love? Didn't that mean anything to him? He spoke as though they were making a business deal, she thought, shivering. Yet what did she want? A pretence of passion? For him to fake a real proposal, sweep her into his arms and tell her lies about loving her? That would be worse, wouldn't it? At least he was being honest; he wasn't trying to deceive her this time.

'You're buying me off, in other words,' she said in a dull, slow voice, and he smiled grimly.

'You could put it that way. But let's just say that I'm offering you a very fair bargain which will suit both of us.'

Anger flared inside her, and she turned away, shaking her head. 'No Mr Garrett, you're wrong. It won't suit me.' She thought of the way his parents had looked at her in their garden yesterday. 'Your mother already thinks I'm a gold-digger,' she said in a husky voice. 'If you married me to stop me bringing the case, she'd be certain of it!'

'Leave my mother to me,' he said coolly. 'I know how to deal with her.'

Belinda looked round at his hard, assured features, the arrogant mouth, the remote eyes, and she shook with a storm of inexplicable emotion, her hands curling into her fists at her sides as she longed to hit him and knock the dry smile off his mouth.

'You know how to deal with everything, don't you? Is that what you promised Ricky and your parents? That you would deal with me, even if you had to marry me to do it? Well, I don't want compensation that badly. In fact, I'm planning to fly to New Zealand to join my family there very soon, and I'll leave my decision about claiming compensation until I've had a chance to talk things over with my mother and stepfather.'

They both heard a little chime of teacups and then Jess appeared with a loaded tray. She gave them both one of her quick, shrewd looks.

'You two aren't squabbling again, are you? Belinda, sit down, do. You mustn't overtire yourself. Vincent, don't be so thoughtless. Leave her alone.' She began to pour tea and Vincent swung away impatiently; he went to stand by the window, staring out, a hand on the frame, his lean body posed with graceful tension, his fingers tapping a terse rhythm on the window.

Belinda threw him a look, couldn't help following the line of his body, and felt her mouth dry suddenly. He was too attractive, damn him.

'Take Belinda her tea,' Jess ordered and he came rather sulkily, his mouth turned down at the corners.

'Oh, I forgot the scones!' Jess said, clicking her tongue, and vanished again. Vincent loomed over Belinda, took her chin between his fingers and forced back her head.

'You aren't going to New Zealand!' he informed her curtly. 'You aren't going anywhere. I want you right under my eyes, where I can make sure you don't cause any more trouble, and, anyway, your family isn't at home at the moment. They've gone on a long camping holiday and won't be back for some weeks.'

Her eyes sharp with suspicion, she stared back. 'How do you know that?'

He shrugged. 'They told me they were leaving.'

'When?' she demanded, watching him with distrust. He always seemed to be a jump ahead of her. Whatever she planned, he had thought of it first and managed to block her.

'I ring them once a week,' he said blandly, and her eyes widened.

'But why? I mean, I didn't realise you knew them. How long have you been doing that?'

'Oh, quite a while. After all, I'm standing in for them!'

'Standing in for them?' She went slightly pink, and he grinned.

'As your family,' he gravely said. 'I've kept in touch with your mother ever since she had to go back to New Zealand, while you were unconscious. She couldn't afford to keep ringing the hospital, so I rang her.'

Belinda bit her lip. 'That was very kind of you,' she said stiffly.

He shrugged. 'I like your mother. I was happy to do it. She's been very worried about you, and she needs a holiday, although she only went when I assured her you would be in the best of hands.' His eyes glinted, and her breathing thickened as she picked up the double meaning.

'I spoke to her recently. Why didn't she tell me they were going away?' she asked crossly.

'I asked her not to. I thought you might feel deserted.'

'Oh.' He was right—knowing that her mother was not at the end of a telephone did disturb her, but how did Vincent guess that? He was such a complicated man; he could be so thoughtful and kind at one minute and so ruthless the next. Would she ever understand him?

'Am I right?' he asked, a smile in his eyes, and she nodded wryly. The smile deepened, and her heart turned over.

Jess bustled back with a plate of scones and put them down. 'Now, do you want butter, or jam and cream, Belinda?' she asked.

'Never mind that,' said Vincent. 'We've got news for you. Belinda and I just got engaged.'

Belinda leapt to her feet. 'Oh! You know I... Why do you...?'

He laughed, grabbing her as she made for the door. 'She's so shy,' he told Jess. 'Look at her, all pink and shaky, like an unset blancmange.'

'Oh, you really are the most——!' hissed Belinda, hitting him and struggling to get away from the arm around her waist.

Jess was too busy exclaiming and beaming to realise what was really going on between them. 'Oh, now, Belinda, don't scold him. I can see he's so excited that he can't keep the secret another minute, and that's wonderful. It means he's really in love.'

Belinda felt her face burn and her breathing stop for a fraction of a second. She looked down, but she knew Vincent was laughing and watching her.

'And I'm not really amazed, you know,' burbled Jess. 'I had my suspicions, I'm not blind!' She smiled, her eyes a little misty. 'I knew something was going on, with Vincent bringing you home, taking such good care of you. I wasn't expecting an engagement this quickly, mind you, but I'm thrilled, both of you, and I hope you're going to be very happy.' She looked at Vincent a little anxiously. 'Have you told your parents yet?'

He solemnly nodded. 'Yes, they know all about it, and they're going to love her when they get to know her.'

'Well, I have,' said Jess a little doubtfully. 'She's a darling, nothing like I'd expected from what your mother said, but...' Her voice tailed off into uneasy silence.

'Look,' Belinda desperately burst out, struggling to get away from Vincent. 'I am not——'

Vincent kissed her and silenced the rest, his arms so tight that she could hardly breathe, and he did not let go of her until they both heard Jess tiptoe out of the room. Then he lifted his head and Belinda furiously glared up at him, green eyes glittering.

'You needn't think you're going to get away with this! I am not marrying you to save your family from paying me damages!'

He was silent for a moment, staring down at her face in a fixed way that made her heart begin to beat like a frantic drummer. 'Maybe it's time I mentioned my other reason for deciding to marry you,' he said at last, his voice light and casual, so that she didn't quite know what to expect yet was wary of him.

'I don't want to hear about it!' she muttered, sure it would all be more lies, and he watched her with an odd intensity, his eyes dark.

'Don't play games, Belinda. You already know, don't you? Women always do know when a man wants them.'

It was like being hit in the stomach; she jerked with shock, hardly able to breathe, and an odd little smile curled his lips. Belinda tried to read that expression, her green eyes unsure and shy. 'Are you saying that . . . that . . . you've fallen in love with me?' she whispered, and his mouth twisted.

'In love? You don't still believe in fairy-tales, do you, Belinda? Come on, we're both adults. I like you a lot, you make me laugh and I enjoy your company, but I'm also a man with a strong sex drive and you are a very beautiful girl. I want to go to bed with you, I think you want to go to bed with me too, but I have a shrewd suspicion I won't get you there if I don't marry you first.'

She felt like bursting into tears, but instead she bit her lip, tasting the metallic tang of her own blood in her mouth. He hadn't been saying he had fallen in love with her at all. Why had she let herself hope that might have been what he meant? A man like Vincent Garrett didn't fall in love with a girl like her. He just amused himself with her—or tried to!

'I don't sleep around!' she bitterly threw at him, trembling.

'That's what I thought you'd say,' he murmured in what sounded like grim satisfaction. 'Not even with Ricky?'

'No! Although if I had it would have been because I loved him, not because I . . . not because . . .'

He laughed, mockery in his eyes. 'Not because you wanted him? So you didn't feel this way about him?'

'This way?' she repeated, face burning. 'I don't know what you mean . . .'

'You know exactly what I mean, Belinda,' he said ruthlessly. 'And if you're still refusing to admit you want me as much as I want you, it's time you faced up to how you really feel.'

'No, don't! I can't bear it!' she whispered hoarsely, trying to evade the hunting mouth, but there was no escape because she might fight him but she could not fight herself. His mouth was as hot as fire and as sweet as honey, and she wanted it so badly that she was dying. She stopped fighting and stood on tiptoe to meet his kiss, her arms going round his neck. They had never kissed like that before. She had not known a kiss could give such wild pleasure. It ran like electricity along all her nerves; it blew her mind, like an overloaded fuse; she shut her eyes and drowned in sensual feeling. Towards the end she could hardly stand up, she was so dizzy, and had to hang on to him to stay on her feet, her face flushed, her eyes as bright as the morning star.

Vincent lifted his head and looked at her again, his eyes glittering and dilated with sensual excitement, and Belinda looked back at him, knowing she must look the same because her body was weak with desire and pleasure.

'Do we understand each other now?' he drawled, and Belinda felt the ache of love in her body with despair.

Surely she hadn't been such a fool as to fall for this man of all men? This was only the second time in her life she had been in love, and for the second time there was going to be no happy ending for her.

She could hardly speak for a moment; she was fighting not to let Vincent see what had happened to her, what he had done to her. She drew a long breath at last and swallowed, looking at him as if from a long, long distance, her pale face cold and contemptuous.

'I have never hated anyone so much in all my life,' she said, and Vincent stared back at her for a moment before he smiled crookedly.

'Well, at least our married life won't be boring for either of us. I'm glad of that.'

CHAPTER NINE

BELINDA didn't believe Vincent meant it, although it would serve him right if she insisted that he did marry her. If she had been the gold-digger he and his family apparently thought she was, that was what she would do! she thought grimly as she dressed the following evening to have dinner with his parents. They would hate it if Vincent married her, of course.

She stepped back to view her reflection in the mirror uncertainly. She wanted to give his parents a better impression of her; it was disturbing to be so disliked. Her old clothes were out of date; fashion moved on fast, and what she had worn happily a year ago looked odd now. Jess had driven her into the nearest town that morning, to do some shopping, and Belinda had spent quite a lot of her savings on new clothes, shoes, lingerie and make-up. She had chosen the dress she was wearing after hunting along rack after rack of clothes. It was a tawny jersey silk; she liked the colour, but even more the way it fitted. She was putting on a little more weight now, but she was still boyishly flat-chested, and she was delighted with the way the dress clung to her small breasts and tiny waist, and gave a smooth line to her slender hips, giving her new curves.

She was very nervous when she went downstairs, and it didn't make her feel any easier to have Vincent's bright, narrowed eyes run down over her in a searching scrutiny. It was like being under a microscope; he didn't miss a thing, from the way she had brushed her copper hair

into light, twisting curls, or had made up her face, with
bronze eye-shadow on her lids and a pinky bronze lipstick, to the way her dress fitted.

His eyes lingered there and she hurriedly sat down,
crossing her legs and trying to look cool and
sophisticated.

'What can I get you to drink?' he asked with a wry
little smile, and she said she would just have a glass of
pineapple juice since they would be drinking wine with
their dinner.

'And you want to keep a clear head?' Vincent mocked.

'I'll need one,' she retorted. 'It isn't going to be a
peaceful evening, and I wish you hadn't arranged this
dinner party. I'm not quite back to normal yet, I look
terrible, your parents don't like me and I'm not
comfortable with them.'

He put her glass into her hand, smiling down at her,
his eyes intimate and warm. 'You look lovely, Belinda,
and my parents won't be able to help liking you once
they get to know you.'

Her face wavered, colour flowing hotly under the skin,
and she couldn't hold his gaze; she had to look away.
It was a relief to hear voices and know that his parents
were arriving. Vincent straightened and turned to greet
them.

'Ah, there you are! Isn't it a wonderful evening? I
thought we were going to have rain for a while, but the
clouds have vanished. Come and say hello to Belinda,
both of you.'

Belinda was on her feet, shyly glancing at them, not
sure what to expect.

'Hello,' his father said gruffly, shaking hands, and his
mother gave her a cold look and a nod without even
offering her hand.

Vincent frowned. 'Sit down, let me get you a drink. Whisky, Dad? Ginger ale in it? Here you are. What about you, Mother? Sherry? A cream sherry, yes, I've got one.'

Belinda sat, dry-lipped, eyes down, wishing she were somewhere else, anywhere else, away from this bleak silence. Vincent poured himself a whisky—a stiffish one, she noticed out of the corner of her eye. Perhaps even Vincent was feeling the strain of this tension?

'How did the meeting go this morning?' his father asked, and Vincent answered smoothly. His mother just sat and looked into her glass. When Vincent stopped speaking another silence fell, and Belinda could not bear any more.

She got to her feet and they all looked quickly at her. Huskily, she said, 'I'll just go and see if they need any help in the kitchen...' then rushed out of the room.

Jess looked round in surprise as she came into the kitchen. 'Don't tell me Vincent's run out of ice already?'

'No, I just came to see if you needed help.'

Jess gave her an understanding smile. 'Don't let Dorothy and Tim scare you. They just need time to get to know you, the way I have! But, while you are here, you can help me carry the smoked duck salad into the dining-room, then we'll tell them to come and sit down.'

'Not just yet!' A new voice behind Belinda made them both start and look round at Mrs Garrett, who stood in the doorway. She said quietly, 'I want a word with Belinda first, please.'

Jess smiled warmly at her. 'Then you can help her carry the first course to the table, Dorothy, and have your little chat in privacy in the dining-room.'

'Thank you, Jess,' Mrs Garrett said with quiet dignity. 'I'll try not to take too long. I don't want to wreck your timing.'

'Don't worry about that, it isn't important, but Belinda is!'

The two women stared at each other; Jess smiled and Mrs Garrett slowly smiled back, nodding. Belinda took a plate in each hand and walked blindly into the dining-room with Mrs Garrett behind her. Was she going to ask her to leave Vincent alone, beg her not to marry him? She felt a curious resentment at the thought of such a request. Of course, she did not want to marry Vincent, yet she was bristling at the idea of his mother's trying to talk her out of it.

'What a pretty table! Jess is such a good house-keeper,' Vincent's mother said. 'This redcurrant sauce looks delicious. I can't remember ever eating smoked duck. Have you, Belinda?'

'No, I don't think so.' Belinda hardly recognised her own voice, it sounded so flat and dull.

Mrs Garrett turned and looked at her ruefully. Her eyes were so like Ricky's, and her silvered hair looked as if it should be artificial because she had a very young face, still unlined, her skin smooth, although she must be in late middle age. 'Belinda, we've upset you, and I'm very sorry. Will you let us try again?' She held out her hand, smiling rather stiffly.

'Of course,' Belinda said politely, shaking hands, then gave her a wry smile. 'Did Vincent ask you to follow me?'

Mrs Garrett laughed, relaxed. 'Yes, he did. How did you guess?'

'It wasn't difficult,' Belinda said with grim amusement. 'He's usually behind everything that happens.'

His mother looked closely at her. 'You sound as if you resent that?'

Belinda drew in her lower lip, sighing. 'Well, he does like his own way, doesn't he?'

'Oh, he does!' Mrs Garrett laughed out loud, her face much more at ease. 'I think his father retired too early and Vincent was very young when he took over the business. My husband had had a slight stroke, you see; oh, it was just a warning, but it scared him into taking things easier, which I was very glad about, but it threw the burden on to Vincent, and he had to toughen up quickly. I'm very proud of the way he coped. It wasn't easy for him, but he dealt with it magnificently. The only trouble is that now he wants to manage everything!'

'I've noticed!' Belinda said, laughing, and Mrs Garrett smiled back.

'He even tries to manage us. When you ran out of the room, he was very angry and almost shouted at us——' She broke off, eyeing Belinda uncertainly, and got a wry little smile of reassurance.

'I can imagine! I'm sorry if he bullied you on my account. You shouldn't have taken any notice of him.'

'Well, my dear, it isn't easy to ignore Vincent, as you obviously know. I won't disguise from you that we were taken aback when we heard he planned to marry you. Oh, nothing personal, we really don't know you, do we? But you see…Vincent tells me that you didn't even know Ricky was engaged before he met you, and you couldn't help what happened, but…well, you have caused a great deal of trouble in our lives, you know. First Ricky's wanting to break with Meg to marry you, which made us very unhappy because we love Meg, and then the accident…such an anxious time. Ricky was beside himself. He thought you would die, and he would be responsible. He couldn't concentrate on his work, he was always going to see you, getting gloomier and gloomier, and we thought he was just going to spend the rest of his life waiting for you to come out of that coma. You can't imagine what a relief it was when he finally accepted that there was no point throwing his life away——' She broke off, looking horrified. 'Oh, my dear! I...that was dreadful of me... I didn't mean...'

Belinda felt like laughing, but it wasn't really funny; tears seemed more appropriate.

'Please, you don't need to explain, I understand how you must have felt,' she said, but Mrs Garrett shook her head, grimacing.

'No, I should watch what I'm saying. I put that very badly. I'm sorry, my dear, I wasn't thinking. You've been through such an ordeal, and I assure you we were all worried about you, and we're very glad you've recovered. I know Ricky is much happier since he saw you. Don't think it was easy for him to... Please believe me, there's nothing personal in the way we feel—after all, we hardly know you. It's just that...well, you have been a sort of catalyst in our lives. Things seem to happen around you. You've brought our family nothing but trouble and it's happening all over again with Vincent. He had promised Ricky to keep an eye on you, but we had no idea it had gone this far—with you living here, I mean. We were thunderstruck when we heard, and then we found out that he was talking of marrying you! It was history repeating itself all over again. I don't suppose he has told you about Magdalen—you met her at our house when you came? We're very fond of her, her family are old friends of ours, and we had all planned that one day... well, we hoped Vincent would marry her, just as we hoped Ricky would marry Meg, and now it seems... well, surely you can understand what a shock it has been?'

She paused, but Belinda couldn't answer. She was too shaken by her own feelings. She wished she knew whether Vincent had meant to marry Magdalen, and whether he was in love with her. But those were hardly questions she could ask his mother.

'You have no need to worry,' she said in a level tone, her face pale. 'I won't be marrying Vincent.'

'You won't?' Mrs Garrett sounded incredulous and looked startled, staring at her as if she couldn't believe what she had just heard.

'No, I won't. So Magdalen can start ordering her wedding dress after all.'

'But Vincent said——'

'Never mind what he said!' Belinda's voice was harsh. 'I am not going to marry him. As soon as I can make the arrangements, I'm flying home to New Zealand. But the dinner will be spoiled if we don't eat it soon, so we'd better go and ask Vincent and your husband to come in to dinner now.'

Eagerly, Mrs Garrett said, 'Don't bother, my dear, you look tired. You sit down, I'll go and fetch them!'

When she had gone, Belinda leaned on a chair, her body drooping and her eyes stinging with unshed tears. She had to get away from here—get away and never see Vincent again. Her heart winced from the thought and a look of appalled admission grew in her green eyes. It hurt so much to think of leaving him that she couldn't be blind to the truth any longer.

She was in love with Vincent Garrett. White-faced, she covered her face with her hands, but hiding did not make the truth go away. It would be there waiting for her however long she hid from it.

The sound of voices and footsteps made her straighten up, her hands dropping from her face, her nerves jumping. She had to pull herself together before he confronted her; Vincent was too shrewd, he saw too much. He had learnt to read her expressions, and he must not read this one.

She forced a smile as the others entered the room. 'Oh, good, you're here. I'm starving!'

Vincent sat down opposite Belinda, eyes hard and narrowed. She avoided meeting his eyes, talking brightly to his mother. 'I'm dying to taste this duck; it looks gorgeous.'

'And the sauce looks even better than the duck,' Mrs Garrett answered cheerfully, taking the seat on the left of her and smiling, although there was anxious curiosity in her eyes as she looked at Belinda's face.

Vincent glanced from one to the other, eyes watchful, then he too smiled and relaxed, taking a bottle of champagne from an ice-bucket. He wrapped a crisp white damask napkin around it and leaned over to pour some into each glass. Belinda couldn't help watching the graceful bend of his body, the formidable angles of his tough face, the gleam of his grey eyes as they met hers. Her heart beat thickly and heavily. I love him, she thought. How did it happen? When did it happen? But how stupid such questions were; what did it matter? There was no such thing as time when you were in love. There was an eternity in a glance, in the touch of a hand.

He smiled at her, and her heart turned over like a landed fish, making her breathless and weak.

He picked up his glass of champagne and tilted it towards her. 'A toast! To us, and our future, Belinda.'

There was a funny little silence, then his parents picked up their own glasses, murmuring inaudibly. Belinda felt the sting of the wine on her tongue, her eyes held by the grey ones, thinking that she would soon have to go away, and wondering how she was going to be able to leave him.

'Now, how about this smoked duck?' Vincent said, putting down his own glass, and she gratefully looked down at her plate.

From then on, the evening took on the unreality of a surrealist dream. She ate beautifully cooked and presented food, she drank champagne, she smiled and talked politely, and kept looking into Vincent's eyes, her head swimming, her body vibrating with a passion she could not control, while underneath all that she was sick with misery because she knew that in a very short time she would be going away and would never see him again.

His parents became much friendlier as the evening wore on and they drank more champagne. The atmosphere had got to them, too. She could almost believe they were beginning to like her, but it was an illusion. Mrs Garrett might be friendly now that Belinda had promised she would never marry their son, but the warmth was a surface one. They would never have accepted her.

They left at around eleven, with Belinda and Vincent waving them off from the door. Vincent calmly slid his arm around Belinda's waist; she felt it there with a plunge of awareness, but waited until his parents were out of sight before she pulled free and turned quickly away.

'Goodnight,' she muttered, eager to escape to bed before she could find herself alone with Vincent, but he caught hold of her shoulder as she fled, smiling down at her with eyes that mocked and told her he knew why she wanted so badly to get away from him.

'It went well, wouldn't you say? I told you my parents would like you once they got to know you. They were just prejudiced. It wasn't really you they disliked—just the idea of any girl coming between Ricky and Meg, and, now they don't have to worry about that, I knew they would soon learn to like you.'

She laughed bitterly. 'Except that now they think I'm coming between you and Magdalen!'

His face tightened, those grey eyes flickering over her own face and away, while he frowned. 'What did my mother say to you when you were alone with her?'

'Oh, you're so quick!' she sneered, her mouth feeling stiff and icy as she tried to laugh.

Vincent's hands slid down from her shoulders to her arms and closed fiercely, his fingertips pressing into her flesh as he shook her. 'What did she tell you?'

'Don't try to bully me, Mr Garrett, because it won't work! She didn't have to tell me anything—I have eyes in my head. I saw the way Magdalen looked at you, so don't try to tell me there's nothing between you, because I wouldn't believe you if you swore it on a stack of bibles.'

He stared down into her angry, uplifted face, his eyes raking over it and making her skin feel raw and ultra-sensitive. 'Forget Magdalen. She has nothing to do with us! I am marrying you, not Magdalen!' he grated, but she saw the harsh angles of his face, heard the hoarse emotion in his voice, and knew that even mentioning the other woman disturbed him. He might plan to marry Belinda in order to end her threat to his family fortunes, and to make sure she did not disturb the equilibrium of Ricky's marriage again, but he was in love with Magdalen, and it wasn't easy for him to act against the dictates of his heart.

'Stop saying that!' she burst out. 'How many times do I have to tell you? I won't marry you! I don't want your money so badly that I could ever forget what you've done to me. I wouldn't marry you if you were the last man on earth!' Her green eyes glittered with defiance, and Vincent's eyes flashed, his face suddenly an alarming mask, taut skin stretched over his bones, eyes slits of white fire, a mouth which had cruelty in every line.

'You will,' he muttered and then his arms were clamped around her, crushing her, making it barely possible to breathe, and her cry of protest was smothered by the hot, relentless possession of his lips. She fought, hands against his chest, pushing, struggling. The kiss was torture to her; she hungered for the touch of his mouth and yet she had to fight it; she couldn't give in to her own desire.

Vincent might want her—she couldn't deny that his body signalled passion, and his lips were fierce and urgent—but desire and love were not the same thing, and Vincent didn't love her; he had coolly said as much, almost amused at the very thought of being in love. He was a man who did not believe in romantic love; it was alien to his vision of the world. He understood desire; he was a man accustomed to pursuing and taking what he wanted. Belinda hated everything about his view of the world—and yet, confusingly, she loved him. She did not understand herself, any more than she understood him.

'Stop fighting it, darling,' he whispered, his lips sliding from her bruised mouth down her throat. 'Oh, Bell, I want you so badly, you don't know...' His hands moved too, touching her with a desire that made her shudder and go weak. He kissed her neck, under her chin, his mouth shaky, his breathing fast. 'I want to take you upstairs, now, and show you how I feel,' he muttered thickly, and she could hardly breathe, her eyes darkly dilated, her body trembling.

'No,' she breathed smokily, lids half-closed, a terrifying weakness stealing over her. He did not love her,
but she loved him, and it split her mind in two to be in
his arms, torn between the two extremes of emotion:
hatred and love. His caresses were a burning temptation
which she didn't know how to fight. She was dying to
surrender to him, put her arms around him, kiss him
back; she needed to touch him intimately, feel his bare
skin under her fingers, discover the male contours of
that body, but she couldn't. She could not let go of her
self-respect or self-control. She was sure Vincent didn't
guess just how deep her feelings were. He might suspect
she was sexually attracted to him—that was something
she could not hide because her body was talking for her
even when she denied it—but if he ever guessed she actually loved him he wouldn't scruple to use her own
feelings against her.

'Not now,' he murmured huskily, and groaned,
burying his mouth on her neck. 'Not yet, Belinda, but
soon... We must be married very soon or I'll go crazy,
wanting you.'

The very idea of it made her go limp, her head buried
on his shoulder, her hands clinging to him, and Vincent
held her very close, his mouth moving on her hair.

'Are you OK?' he asked with sudden anxiety, putting
a hand under her chin to tilt her face towards him.

She blinked in the light, her lashes fluttering, hiding
her expression from his searching gaze. 'I'm very tired,
that's all.'

'Why didn't you remind me? I'm sorry, I keep forgetting how frail you still are... Come on, I'll carry you
to bed.'

'No,' she cried out, too late, as he put an arm under
her legs and lifted her off the ground, into his arms.

He smiled down at her and she could almost have believed the curve of that mouth held tenderness, except that she knew her eyes deceived her.

'No argument! I don't want you cracking up before our wedding day.' He carried her up the stairs, held close to him, her hair spilling over his sleeve, her eyes closed because she knew he was watching her and she did not want to meet his gaze.

'Shall I help you undress?' he teased as he laid her down on the bed, and she went pink. Vincent laughed softly. 'I love it when you turn shy and blush. Goodnight, Bell.' He knelt beside the bed and took her hand, turned it upward and lingeringly kissed the palm, making her tremble and shiver.

She couldn't resist touching his dark hair; her fingers felt the thick filaments clinging to her skin, and she heard Vincent sigh, then he was on his feet and gone and she was alone. She slowly got up and undressed, her body quite disorientated, cold and shaking one minute, feverish the next, her fingers all thumbs, catching in clothes, fumbling with buttons and zips.

She didn't think she would ever sleep, and indeed she slept badly, falling asleep at around two in the morning, and awakening again at seven, although she did not get up until eight. She stayed in bed until then because she did not want to see Vincent at breakfast and knew he left before eight o'clock.

'You look wan,' said Jess, frowning, and Belinda made up some story about having a headache. Jess took her through her usual exercise routine, though, and that put some more colour into Belinda's face. Just as they finished, the phone rang. Jess took the call and came back looking rather harassed.

'That was Vincent,' she said, and Belinda's heart skipped a beat. 'The hospital just got in touch with him, asking if you could switch your appointment with the specialist. He has to fly to Tokyo unexpectedly and he'll be there for at least a week, so he won't be there tomorrow, when you were to see him for your check-up, but he could fit you in this afternoon. Vincent says it's vital that you see the doctor to make sure your progress is satisfactory, so he asked me to drive you up to London.'

Belinda's eyes widened. 'Right away?'

'I'm afraid so.' Jess looked at her with an uncertain expression. 'Unfortunately, I promised to help the vicar's wife with the Sale of Work this afternoon, but Vincent said that if I drive you up to London he'll bring you home, so that I can just drop you there and come straight back.'

Belinda slowly thought aloud. 'You'll leave me at the hospital?'

'Is that all right, or would you rather I stayed with you until Vincent arrived?' Jess looked anxiously at her, and Belinda hurriedly shook her head.

'Of course I can manage on my own. I'm a big girl now.' She smiled and Jess laughed in relief.

'Thank you, Belinda. You'll have a bit of a wait to see the doctor, I'm afraid, because he is rushing to squeeze a lot of appointments in this afternoon, but Vincent promised to get there at four-thirty prompt. He says you're to wait in the hospital foyer for him.'

'I'll be fine,' Belinda said absently, her throat tightening as she realised that this gave her the opportunity she needed. If she saw the doctor early enough, she might be able to leave before Vincent arrived, get a taxi to a hotel, and book the first available flight to New Zealand.

'You'd better change quickly, and take a shower, then we'll go,' Jess said, looking at her watch, and Belinda went obediently to her room, her mind very busy as she dressed in one of her new outfits. She couldn't pack any of her clothes. She couldn't take much with her, or it would arouse Jess's suspicions, but she made sure she had money, her cheque-book and passport. They would have to send on all her other possessions. It didn't matter. She could buy what she needed once she was safely in London and out of Vincent's reach.

Jess looked rather oddly at her as they drove out of the gates several hours later. 'You aren't running a temperature, are you? You look a little feverish.'

'I'm excited by going to London, I suppose,' Belinda lied smoothly, and Jess smiled.

'Well, calm down before you see the doctor or he'll have you back in hospital!'

Belinda took a deep breath, ironically realising how right Jess was, but for very different reasons. She must look cool and casual, even while she was saying goodbye to Jess at the hospital entrance, which would be hard because she was going to miss Jess badly, but the last thing she wanted to do was arouse suspicion. If she was to get away she had to make sure nobody so much as guessed at her intentions.

While they drove along the motorway into London, her mind was busy with all the things she had to do before she got on that plane to New Zealand. She would get a taxi to Oxford Street, do some rapid shopping, buy a suitcase, then take another taxi and check into one of the large, anonymous airport hotels before she rang up and booked her flight. It sounded very simple, but she knew it would be a fraught period for her before she actually boarded her plane, because she couldn't hope to get away without Vincent catching up with her at some point. With luck, that would be in the actual airport when she was boarding her plane, and he could hardly do much in a Heathrow terminal! Or could he? Her mind ran riot imagining the scene, and she felt her stomach churning violently.

'Here we are,' Jess said cheerfully, pulling up outside the London hospital entrance, and Belinda came out of her own thoughts, her eyes blinking in surprise.

'Oh, yes . . . so we are.' She looked up at the hospital, reluctant to get out of the car, to go in there again. This place had been where she spent eight months of her life without even being aware of it, and she hated the memory of those months. 'Well . . . goodbye, Jess . . . and . . . thank you . . .' Her voice broke slightly and she caught the look of surprise on Jess's face, which made her pull herself together. She smiled somehow. 'It was good of you to drive me up here; sorry about the trouble I've caused. I hope you get back in time to help the vicar's wife, and . . . thanks . . .'

She dived out of the car and almost ran into the hospital, conscious of Jess's staring after her with a puzzled expression, and angry with herself for losing control like that. She had meant to be calm and collected, and she had been nothing of the kind, but it wasn't easy to say goodbye to Jess, who had been so kind to her.

It wasn't going to be easy to leave this country and know she would never see Vincent again, either, but she had no other option. Leaving him was better than marrying him, knowing he did not love her.

CHAPTER TEN

THERE were butterflies in Belinda's stomach as she left the hospital just over an hour later, and hurried towards the taxi-rank outside the entrance. Vincent had said he would get there at four-thirty, it was just after four, and she was terrified that he might be early and catch her before she could escape.

It was a cool afternoon, with the sun behind clouds and a threat of rain in the air which no doubt was why she was shivering despite the light summer raincoat Jess had made her wear, in case it did rain. As she reached the first taxi in the line, Belinda threw a furtive glance over her shoulder, feeling like a fugitive on the run from the police.

'Yes, miss?' The voice made her jump and look round, paling, then flushing as she met the quizzical eyes of the taxi-driver.

'Oh, yes… Can you take me to Oxford Street, please?' she said huskily, climbing into the back of the cab.

'You'll be cutting it a bit fine,' the driver said, starting his engine.

Puzzled, she stared, and he turned his head to grin at her.

'By the time we get there it will be nearly closing time for most of the shops!'

'Oh…yes. Could you take me to Selfridges, then?'

'Good thinking. Get it all under one roof,' said the driver, settling back comfortably as they pulled up at traffic lights. 'You visiting someone in the hospital, were you?'

Belinda inwardly groaned—was he going to talk to her all the way to Oxford Street? Just her luck, to get a chatty taxi-driver when what she wanted to do was think.

'No, I had a check-up there,' she flatly responded, and the driver said he hoped she was OK.

'Yes, I'm fine now,' she said, and he cheerfully began telling her a lengthy anecdote about an illness he had had the previous year, from which he plunged into a description of his own hospital stay, the details of his operation and what the surgeon had said to him.

The lights changed and the taxi started off again, passing a line of traffic queuing to move in the opposite direction towards the hospital. Out of the corner of her eye Belinda suddenly caught a familiar gleam and her head spun. Vincent's car! There was no mistaking the beautiful thing. She had escaped just in time. He was ten minutes early. He was behind the wheel, his head in profile to her, and she stared at that tough, lean face hungrily, aching with pain, but at least she was getting the chance to see him one more time, even if she couldn't actually say goodbye.

At that instant, as if feeling her gaze on him, he turned his head, and their eyes would have met if Belinda hadn't moved hurriedly along the seat of the taxi, out of his eyeline. She was shaking, and wanted to cry, but her driver was watching her curiously in his mirror, so she couldn't give in to her tears.

'You OK, miss?' he asked, and she nodded, forcing a false, bright smile.

Just then they both heard the loud blare of car horns, shouting, a grinding of brakes and a screech of tyres.

'What's that silly fool doing?' the taxi-driver said to himself, peering into his wing mirror. 'He knows he can't turn round there!'

Belinda's heart almost stopped. Turning round? She did not dare risk a backward glance. It couldn't be... it mustn't be Vincent!

'Look at him!' invited her driver, staring fixedly into his mirror. 'A U-turn in the middle of a main road with all this traffic around. Out of his mind. I don't know, some of these drivers! Think they own the road! London's a crazy place these days. Sometimes I'm so worn out when I get home after a day's driving around that I can hardly manage a word with my wife, and you should hear what she has to say. Change your job, she says, get out of London, she says, give yourself a break, let's go and live in the country, but it's all very well for her to talk like that, but what would I do in some village? All I know is driving a taxi...'

Belinda let his words wash over her while she screwed her head round to look through the rear window at the road behind them. She spotted Vincent's car immediately, coming after them at a dangerous pace, weaving around other vehicles, ignoring their hoots of indignation and rage.

He's going to catch up with us! she thought, panic making her shake, but then the taxi passed through another set of traffic lights just as they were about to turn red, and, looking back anxiously, she saw that Vincent had been forced to stop. She could almost hear his irritation.

'Can you take a short cut?' she asked her driver, leaning forward and managing a convincing little smile. 'I'm in such a hurry to get my shopping done before the shops shut.'

'I'm doing my best!' the man said, offended. 'I'll try down here, though—sometimes it isn't quite so busy in these back streets.' He took a sudden right turn, into a side-street, and lapsed into silence while she sat back in her seat again, mouth dry, hands clenched, praying that Vincent hadn't spotted that change of direction.

A few minutes later the taxi pulled up at the side entrance of Selfridges department store and Belinda climbed hurriedly out, paid the driver and bolted into the shop. A backward glance told her that there was no sign of Vincent. She had shaken him off.

She rushed through the store, buying the bare essentials—some underwear, a couple of nightdresses, a dressing-gown, a skirt and several tops, stockings, and finally a cheap suitcase. She could buy other things when she safely reached New Zealand, but there were definitely advantages to travelling light.

She had difficulty getting another taxi because the evening homeward rush had begun and all the taxis seemed occupied, but eventually she got one outside the Selfridges hotel, next door to the store, and an hour later she was in a hotel within five minutes of the airport.

She rang to book a flight as soon as she was in her room, and was deeply relieved to be told there was a seat available on a plane next day. She tried to ring home again, but there was still no reply. She would have to go to a hotel when she got to New Zealand, until her family came home, but at least she would be out of Vincent's reach there. He wouldn't follow her all that way!

She sank back on her bed, sighing with exhaustion after the rush to get here. She was sticky with heat and felt grubby after all those hours in London's grimy, petrol-laden air. What she needed was a shower and some clean clothes.

She had a leisurely shower, then towelled herself and put on one of the new nightdresses she had bought; very short, ending at her knee, it was crisp white cotton, with lace frills at the scooped neckline and tiny puff sleeves. She realised when she looked at herself in the mirror that the nightdress was transparent when she had light behind her, so she put on the matching dressing-gown.

Wandering back into the bedroom, she looked at her watch and was surprised to realise that it was nearly half-past seven. No sooner had she registered the time than it triggered her body clock and she felt hungry, but she couldn't be bothered to get dressed again, and anyway, she was wary of being seen, even inside the hotel, so she decided not to go down to the restaurant but to order from room service. She sat down and studied the menu propped up on the table by the window, chose melon cocktail followed by salmon mayonnaise with salad, and a pot of coffee, then rang her order through.

While she was waiting, she found an electric hairdrier provided by the management, and began to blow-dry her hair. The whine of the little motor drowned out all other sounds, which was why she did not at first hear the knocking on the door until it became quite loud. When the sound did penetrate, she rushed to let the waiter in, but when the door swung open it wasn't a waiter with her meal who pushed his way into the room, it was Vincent.

Belinda gave a gasp of shock, and tried to close the door before he was quite through it, then tried to push him out again, but he was far too strong for her. It was useless. He dealt with her by the simple expedient of putting an arm around her to clamp her arms to her side, and lifted her bodily off the floor, struggling and muttering wordlessly, then he kicked the door shut with a backward slam of one foot, walked with her across the room and dropped her on the bed.

She lay there, breathless, her heart thudding, staring up at him while he stood beside the bed, staring back, his brows very black and jagged above brooding eyes.

'Now, what the hell do you think you're doing?' he asked harshly.

'I was just going to ask you the same thing!' she snapped back.

'Belinda! Don't try my patience!' he snarled, bending towards her with his hands curling at his sides as if he wanted to hit her. 'I've spent the last few hours hunting London for you, and I'm very tired and very fed up, so I advise you not to make me any angrier than I already am!'

Her curiosity got the better of her and she had to ask him. 'How did you find me?'

'I got your taxi's number and rang his headquarters, who contacted him and asked where he had dropped you. I went to Selfridges, but of course you had left by the time I got there. I rushed around the store like a scalded cat until I managed to find someone who remembered you, a man who had sold you a suitcase, and that made it obvious you were running away.'

'I am not running away! I'm going home to be with my family!' she said stiffly. 'I miss them, and now that I'm so much better I want to be with them, not living with strangers.'

Vincent turned sardonic eyes on her. 'So you bolted without a word to Jess, let alone me? All right, you didn't feel you could bear to say goodbye to me, but didn't Jess deserve better treatment? Wouldn't it have been polite to thank her for everything she has done for you? Didn't it occur to you that she would be deeply upset if you had just vanished without a word? How was anyone to know what had happened to you? You could have been abducted, murdered...anything might have happened.'

She looked down, flushing. 'I hadn't thought...I'd have rung Jess once I was in New Zealand...written, anyway——'

'By which time Jess would have been quite distraught, and no doubt we would have contacted the police. We would have had to! You must have known that you couldn't just vanish. I don't suppose for a moment that your specialist would consider you ready for a long flight like that, anyway. You are still undergoing treatment; you're not fit yet. But you knew all that—and you didn't care, did you? You were running as fast and as far as you could——'

'No!' she protested thickly, unable to look at him.

'Yes!' he bit out. 'We both know you're running away, and we both know why—you're scared out of your wits because you can't handle the way you feel about me.'

She felt unbearable, intolerable pain and would have run away then if she had had anywhere to run to or any hope of getting away from him. 'All I feel for you is contempt!' she muttered, her head averted.

He ignored her, his voice cutting. 'Ricky was a very safe man to love, wasn't he? It was all a lovely, rosy glow, a fairy romance—holding hands in the moonlight stuff, sex didn't come into it. A few lingering kisses would be as far as you went. Ricky isn't very highly sexed, he's been too spoilt to have any really strong feelings about anyone but himself, so he wouldn't have made any dangerous demands on you. But you know it will be different with me, and you can't face it.'

Face burning, trembling with anger and resentment, she shouted at him. 'What I can't face is the very thought of having to live with you any longer! Your vanity may prefer to believe that I fancy you, but you couldn't be more wrong. I can't bear it when you touch me. It makes me sick——' She broke off with a gasp of panic as Vincent lunged at her, face tense, eyes glittering.

'Get away from me!' she cried, scrambling backwards to get away, but found herself up against the bedhead. His hands fastened on her, pulling her towards him; his arm went round her back and arched her body to meet his kiss. His mouth was so hot that she felt it almost scorched her; her lips quivered helplessly under that insistent possession, and then weakly parted, despite her desperate attempt not to give in to him. Vincent made a husky little sound, almost a groan, and Belinda felt tears sting under her closing lids. She couldn't deny the need, the desire, any more. Her body was rioting, in defiant rebellion too strong for her.

'Oh, Bell,' he muttered, a hand at her waist, untying the yellow ribbons fastening her dressing-gown. She slid her arms around his neck, clenched her hands in his dark hair, wanting him with a terrible hunger. His hand unbuttoned the neckline of her nightie; his fingertips slid over her bare breast and Belinda moaned, moving feverishly against him.

'Tell me you want me,' he whispered, his palm cupping the warm flesh he had uncovered. He was lying on the bed with her now, almost on top of her; he lowered his head and she gave a wild cry of pleasure as she felt his tongue-tip teasing and caressing her nipples. 'Stop fighting it, Bell. What are you afraid of? Tell me...'

'I can't...' she groaned. 'Don't make me, Vincent. This isn't how I want it to be.'

He lay with his head on her breast, his face warm on her, his dark hair falling like feathers on her white flesh, tickling her. 'How do you want it to be, Bell? Just tell me and I'll make it happen.'

But he didn't understand; he had never understood. He had suspected and despised her from the beginning, and nothing had changed. He thought she was talking about money again, probably. He was so wrong about her. He thought she was scared of sex, when all she was scared of was sex with a man who didn't love her, because that would destroy her; she was terrified of the temptation to give in because afterwards she might hate him, but she would also hate herself.

'I want love,' she sobbed, her eyes shut and the slow tears crawling down her face.

Vincent arched himself over her; she felt his staring, but was afraid to open her eyes to see his expression. What was he thinking? Was he wondering whether to lie? Did he think she wouldn't know he was lying?

'And you can never give it to me,' she said in sudden weariness, the tears wet on her cheek.

Vincent bent down suddenly; she felt his mouth touch the trail of the tears, felt his tongue lick the salt on her skin, then he began to kiss her softly, quick little kisses fluttering down her face from her wet eyes to her mouth where his lips stayed, became fierce and demanding, pushing her mouth open, merging with her.

Their intense concentration on each other was abruptly broken as somebody knocked loudly on the door. They jumped apart, eyes startled. Vincent lifted his head, scowling. 'What the hell——? Who can that be?'

'My dinner,' she said, half laughing, half on the verge of tears. 'I rang room service just before you arrived. I thought you were the waiter with my dinner when you knocked.'

Vincent let go of her, grimacing, as the waiter called, 'Room service!' and knocked again.

'I suppose we'd better let him in before he uses his pass key!' he said grimly, and walked towards the door.

Belinda slid rather unsteadily off the bed and tidied her hair, then tied her dressing-gown belt again with shaking hands. There was a mirror on the wall opposite; she gave her reflection a hurried glance, horrified by her appearance. She was flushed, confused, dishevelled. She looked like a woman who had been caught making love, which was, of course, exactly what she was!

'Your meal, sir,' the waiter said, gliding in with the food arranged on a wheeled table. He gave Belinda a surprised and curious look, then glanced at the food. 'The order was just for one person, wasn't it, sir?'

'Only one of us is eating,' Vincent said, handing him a handsome tip. 'Thank you.'

The waiter bowed, 'Thank you, sir. Goodnight.' He smiled smoothly. 'Goodnight, madam.' The door closed behind him and Belinda gave a low groan.

'Goodness only knows what he thought!'

'Oh, it was obvious what he thought, but who cares?' Vincent lifted the silver cover from her meal. 'Sit down and eat your meal.'

'Will you stop ordering me around?' she flared, turning on him, and he raised an eyebrow.

'It was mere common sense. You're obviously hungry.'

'I was, until you arrived!'

'Sit down and eat, Bell, and don't be tiresome.' He walked towards the telephone on the bedside table. 'I'm going to ring Jess. She must be frantic with worry by now.'

'You haven't told her——?' she began, and broke off as he turned those sardonic eyes on her.

'I rang to tell her not to expect us back for a few hours,' he said drily. 'I decided not to upset her by telling her that you had run away until I'd found you and we were on our way back.'

She froze. 'I am not coming back!'

'Oh, yes, you are,' he coolly told her, picking up the phone and beginning to dial.

'I am flying to New Zealand tomorrow!' she insisted.

'Eat your dinner!' was all Vincent said in reply to that.

She fizzed with resentment at his tone, but before she could react he asked, 'What did the specialist say, by the way? Jess is bound to ask.'

'He said I was progressing amazingly well.'

'Good,' he said, then began talking into the phone. 'Hello, Jess. Yes, it's me again. Look, don't wait up for us. We've decided to have dinner somewhere special, to celebrate, and I don't think it would be a good idea for Belinda to face a long drive back afterwards, so we're going to take a couple of rooms in a hotel for the night. We'll drive back tomorrow after breakfast.' He paused to listen, then said, 'Oh, she's fine, yes. A clean bill of health from the hospital.' Another pause, and he smiled, then stopped smiling as Jess said something else. 'What did you tell her?' Vincent asked sharply.

Belinda sat down and began to eat her melon cocktail, not really aware of what she was eating, her eyes and all her attention on Vincent. She couldn't see his face; he had his back to her now. She watched with passion the lean, elegant line of his body, the strongly shaped head, the black hair which just brushed his white collar, the way the long, powerful fingers tapped impatiently on the bedside table as he listened to Jess.

'I see,' he said with curt irritation. 'Well, if she rings again, just say I'm away and you don't know when I'll be back.'

Belinda knew he was talking about Magdalen and jealousy hit her like a blow in the stomach. She stared down at her food fixedly.

'Yes, thanks, we will,' Vincent said. 'Goodnight, Jess.' He put the phone down and turned back towards her.

She made herself go on eating, but what she put in her mouth might as well have been sawdust.

'Jess sends her love and hopes we enjoy the evening,' Vincent said.

'You're so plausible!' muttered Belinda. 'But how are you going to convince Magdalen that you've got to marry me instead of her? What do you plan to do about her if I do marry you? A little love-nest somewhere? If she's as crazy about you as everyone seems to think, maybe she'll settle for that, but I know I wouldn't. Magdalen may have more self-respect than you bargain for! Even if you can persuade her you still love her, she could start to hate you for preferring money to her!'

Vincent watched her, a gleam in his eye, his mouth curling at the edges. 'You don't need to be jealous of Magdalen——' he began and she furiously interrupted, a red spot in each cheek.

'Don't kid yourself! I'm not jealous of her!'

'Because I've never been in love with her,' Vincent coolly carried on over her angry voice, and she stopped to stare at him intently. He smiled at her. 'It was just a stupid idea our families had—my mother and her mother, largely, plotting together, matchmaking, day-dreaming. Oh, I used to see quite a bit of Magdalen; it was inevitable, since my family was so friendly with hers. I often ended up as her partner at theatre trips and dinner parties. We were thrown together, but on my side it was never a love-affair.'

Belinda watched him. 'On her side it was, though,' she quietly stated, and he shrugged, his mouth wry.

'Maybe, or maybe she just liked the idea of being my wife. I am quite wealthy and she would have a very comfortable life as my wife.'

Belinda laughed angrily. 'You're so modest. She isn't in love with you, just your money? Not very nice, is it? If I were Magdalen, I'd hate you for putting it like that.'

'I didn't mean that exactly,' he said with impatience, glowering at her. 'She wouldn't put it like that to herself. Her family have money, too. But I am the sort of husband Magdalen would be expected to marry. I've never felt she was in love with me, only with the idea of being my wife.' He gave her a sideways look, mockery in his face. 'But if I hadn't met you, I might have ended up marrying Magdalen one day, when I had given up hoping.'

'Hoping?' she whispered, her heart racing, and he smiled down into her eyes.

'Hoping to meet someone I could really love,' he said softly, and Belinda could scarcely breathe. She dared not believe it; he was such a smooth liar, so plausible and convincing, and yet when he looked at her like that she almost did believe it, and she wanted to so much.

'Don't lie to me!' she cried out, and Vincent took her hands and drew her to her feet, holding her hands flattened against his chest.

'Can you feel my heart beating?' he murmured, and she could; the heavy thud of his heartbeat came up through her palms, but what did that prove? She looked frowningly at him, shaking her head.

'You told me falling in love just happened in fairy-stories. You said adults didn't believe in it. You said——'

'I said a damn sight too much!' he interrupted irritably.

'But you did say it, and you meant it!'

'Half meant it,' he said, his mouth twisting, and she watched him with painful uncertainty and an even more painful hope because she wanted to believe him, but she was afraid of getting hurt again. Vincent said slowly, 'How can I make you understand? It isn't so long since you were madly in love with Ricky. When you first came out of the coma you were still in love with him. I didn't want to make a fool of myself by telling you I was in love with you if you were still fixated on my brother. I was sure by then that you found me attractive, that was obvious——'

'Oh, was it?' she muttered, very flushed, and he smiled at her with sudden tenderness.

'Yes, you know it was, my darling. You and I are very compatible, sexually speaking—and I thought we could base a marriage on that for a start, but I wasn't ready to admit I loved you until I could hope that you felt the same way.'

'You wanted to marry me to stop me bringing a case against Ricky!'

'I wanted to marry you because I was afraid some other man might appear in your life if I didn't!' Vincent said drily. 'You were talking about going back to New Zealand and I couldn't bear the idea. Oh, I'd have followed you if you had gone, but I was desperate to think of a way of stopping you, of keeping you with me.'

'So that I shouldn't sue Ricky!' she said, watching him and wishing she could be sure he was telling the truth.

He put a hand under her chin and tilted her head right back. 'Look at me, my darling,' he said in a deep, husky voice, and she looked into those grey eyes and wondered how she had ever thought that they were cold, because they were nothing of the kind; they had a fire burning in them, a dark, consuming fire in which she saw herself reflected, her tiny image thrown on to the black pupils of his eyes.

'I love you to the point of desperation,' he said unsteadily, and Belinda gave a husky little moan, swaying towards him.

'Vincent!'

Their mouths met with an explosive force, and her arms went round his neck. For that moment she refused to think, to doubt, to feel uncertainty. She had to believe the passion and tenderness she felt in him now.

'Tell me,' he pleaded against her yielding mouth. 'Tell me you love me, too, my darling.'

'I love you,' she breathed out and her heart beat even faster as she heard his groan of satisfaction.

He sank backwards on the bed, holding her on his lap, kissing her so urgently that she was almost suffocated, and she hung limply from his shoulders as if she would fall if she let go of him, her long, coppery hair tumbling down her back. Vincent's hand wound through the soft strands, stroking and playing with them. His other hand was making her head swim as it slid under her nightie and explored her naked body, upwards from her parted thighs, a lingering journey to the warm globes of her breasts. He was breathing as if he had run a marathon and she felt the shudder of desire rising in him as steeply as it rose in her.

She pulled back from his mouth, breathlessly whispering, 'I must breathe sometimes, Vincent!'

His colour was dark, his eyes feverish. 'Sorry, you just blew my mind,' he muttered, staring down at the surrendered curve of her body. 'You drive me crazy, did I tell you? Just to see you walk into a room makes my temperature shoot up. You are so lovely, my darling. I love everything about you, from your gorgeous hair to your sexy little body.'

'Skinny little body,' she said wistfully, leaning on him, her head pillowed on his shoulder. 'When did you start thinking you might be falling in love?' she asked, fiddling with his tie, undoing it, pulling it off.

'I fell in love with you slowly, day by day, when I sat beside your bed in the hospital,' he said in a low, husky voice. 'Oh, Ricky came too, at first, but he couldn't bear it. He hated seeing you lying there; it made him uneasy. It reminded him that he was still walking around, and it made him guilty, so he would come in and look at you and then bolt.'

'Poor Ricky!' she said with tolerance, because it no longer mattered to her that Ricky was weak.

Vincent looked impatient. 'Poor Ricky?' he repeated, frowning. 'Didn't you hear what I just said? He ran out on you when you needed him, although he was driving when you were injured. Don't call him poor Ricky to me! If you had married him, you'd spend the rest of your life acting as his mother. It is going to be Meg who looks after Ricky, not the other way around, you know.'

'I worked that out,' she admitted.

'I thought you had by now,' he said, smiling crookedly. 'Why do you think I stopped being jealous of Ricky?'

'Were you jealous?' she asked, her heart beating very fast as she watched him through her lashes, a half-smile curving her lips.

'Jealous as hell,' he said shortly, his face darkening, then he looked down at her and laughed. 'But not any more, so take that complacent look off your face!'

She laughed. 'You've no need to be jealous of Ricky. When I saw him again, at your parents' house, I realised he didn't mean a thing to me any more. I had fallen out of love without even realising it. I might have known earlier if I hadn't seen you all the time and constantly been reminded of Ricky. After all, it had been months since I'd set eyes on him, but I had been seeing you quite often.' She frowned, a thought occurring to her. 'Why did you come to see me in the hospital every day? You didn't cause the accident, you had no need to feel guilty; why did you visit me?'

He made a wry little face. 'Oh, well, I suppose I always rather fancied you, from the beginning. I was furious because Ricky wanted to marry you, and I was angry with you, too, but after the accident I went along to see you the first time because Ricky couldn't face going alone, and he begged me to come. After I'd seen you lying there like Snow White, fast asleep in a modern version of the glass casket, all hooked up to a life-support machine, I felt guilty, because I'd opposed the idea of Ricky's marrying you, and you lay there looking so lost and so lovely, and so lifeless.'

'Snow White,' she said dreamily. 'I like that. It sounds a lot nicer than just being in a coma. Snow White in a glass casket...' She gave him a teasing look. 'But are you the prince—or one of the seven dwarfs?'

He laughed. 'Which do you want me to be?'

'Oh, the prince, I think. Ricky can be a dwarf.' She thought for a moment, then asked curiously, 'What did he think of your daily visits to me? Wasn't he surprised?'

'No, he was grateful. He thought I was doing it for him, to save him having to go. Ricky always does see things from his own exclusive point of view. My mother didn't like it, though. It didn't occur to her that I had fallen in love with you. She just thought I was obsessed, and of course I was, if you can call love an obsession. It was that sort of feeling for me because you just lay there and didn't even know I was there. She's shrewd, my mother, and she knows me very well. She knew I couldn't stay away from you. She thought it was unhealthy for me to be sitting there day after day just staring at you and talking to you while you were totally oblivious of me.'

Belinda was pale, her imagination presenting her with a vivid image of him sitting beside her in that stark little hospital room, talking to her while she was quite unaware of him. It brought it all back to her, the shock of waking up to find she had lost so many months of her life, that the world had spun round for eight months without her knowing it.

She shook off the grey web of memories, shivering. 'You talked to me, too? I know the nurses did, they told me about it afterwards, and I wondered if I could really hear them, even though I was unconscious, because it was so odd that I woke up on Ricky's wedding day! It can't be a coincidence, can it? I must have heard them talking about it; it must have been such a shock that it made me wake up. What else explains how I came out of the coma on that very day?'

Vincent stared at her, his face tense and pale too. 'It was me,' he said.

Belinda frowned, her eyes fixed on him. 'You? What do you mean?'

'I told you. I came that morning, very early, and sat with you for an hour to tell you.'

She was too thunderstruck to say anything and Vincent grimaced ruefully.

'God knows why I did it. I never told Ricky I had— but I felt I had to. I'd got into the habit of telling you everything that happened to me, everything I had on my mind. It was so easy to talk to you; it was like confession, talking into the dark. I sat and talked and, although you just lay there, I often felt that you could hear me and were listening. I never talked about Ricky, though, and I didn't tell you he was going to marry Meg. But on the wedding day, I woke up and I knew I had to tell you. I hadn't meant to go to the hospital because it was going to be a hectic day and I had so much to do, but something forced me to go. I felt guilty, I suppose, because I wanted Ricky to marry Meg not you, and you lay there in that other world, far away from all of us. I had to tell you, so I did, and I felt you were listening. It was such a strong feeling, Belinda. I'm sure I didn't imagine it. I could feel you listening . . . and when they rang and told me you had recovered consciousness just a few hours later, I knew it had to be because I'd told you Ricky was getting married. I knew I'd broken into that glass casket and woken Snow White up, but you had woken up for Ricky, not me, and my God! I was jealous about that!'

'Why didn't you tell me this before?' For some reason she couldn't quite fathom, it seemed vitally important. That it should be Vincent who had brought her back into life! Vincent who had sat and talked to her day after day! If she had ever doubted his love for her, she did not doubt it now. Eight months of visiting her every day without ever getting a sign of life from her? It stunned her.

'How could I tell you without betraying the rest of it?' he said flatly. 'I wasn't ready to talk about my daily visits to you. I warned the hospital staff not to blurt it out, either. They agreed with me that it would be wiser not to tell you too much at first. Nobody knew what effect the coma had had on you . . .'

She whitened, biting her lip. 'You all thought I might be crazy!'

Vincent flinched. 'Of course not! My God, my darling, of course we didn't think . . .' But his eyes didn't quite meet hers and she smiled with grim humour.

'Do you think I wasn't afraid of it, too? Do you think it hasn't haunted me day and night since I woke up . . . the fear of going mad, of what damage had been done to my brain? I even thought that that was why I was so attracted to you!'

He laughed harshly. 'Well, thanks! So you thought you had to be crazy to be attracted to me, did you?'

She gave him a wry, passionate look. 'Is that surprising? I started out by hating you, but kept finding myself kissing you. Of course I thought I was acting very oddly! When you hate someone you don't generally keep falling into their arms.'

Vincent's face softened; his grey eyes held tender amusement. 'Don't you? I thought you did. You certainly have lately.' He held her closer. 'And what about sitting on someone's knee? What is that a sign of? Loathing? Or that you're going to marry them very soon?'

Belinda touched his cheek with one hand, sighing. 'Darling, I can't . . . your mother dislikes me, she told me frankly that she didn't want me as a daughter-in-law, and how can I marry you when it will mean quarrelling with your family?'

'My mother won't quarrel with me. None of them will. Don't worry, she doesn't know you well enough yet.

When she does, she'll soon get used to the idea of you as a daughter-in-law.'

'What if she doesn't?' Belinda asked grimly.

'She'll have to,' Vincent said with terse force. 'I am going to marry you, whatever anyone thinks. I'm not risking my happiness by letting my family interfere with my life!'

'Oh, but, Vincent——' Belinda began, and he put a finger on her lips, silencing her.

'No argument. It upsets you, and I won't have you getting upset. You look pale already.' He frowned down at her. 'Are you feeling tired? Maybe you should go to bed and get some rest?'

'I'm fine,' she protested.

'Hmm...' His eyes wandered to the table. 'Your dinner! You haven't eaten that. You probably have low blood-sugar. You must eat it right away.'

He put her on her feet and stood up himself, watching with a teasing smile as she retied her dressing-gown and ran shaky hands over her ruffled hair. 'You look wonderful, don't worry!' he told her. 'Sit down and eat your dinner. That coffee will be stone-cold, and you shouldn't be drinking coffee at this time of night, anyway. I wonder if there is wine in the mini bar over there?'

She sat down at the table, her hunger returning suddenly, while Vincent went to check on the contents of the bar. He came back with a bottle of white wine, which he opened and poured into two glasses while she was eating her salad. It was an enormous meal—far too much for her—and she offered some to Vincent. He grinned.

'Why not? That's what marriage is all about, isn't it? Sharing?'

They only had one fork so they both used it, feeding each other, smiling into each other's eyes. The wine went to Belinda's head, or was it Vincent? Whatever the cause, she felt dizzy and light-headed; she felt like a balloon soaring far above the earth.

'Happy, darling?' Vincent asked, and she nodded, beyond words, but it didn't matter, she didn't need words with Vincent. He knew how she felt, and looking into his smiling grey eyes, she knew how he felt, too, and at last she had no doubts, no fears. She was utterly certain now. They belonged together.

Take 4 bestselling love stories FREE

Plus get a FREE surprise gift!

HARLEQUIN®
OFFICIAL SWEEPSTAKES
RULES

NO PURCHASE NECESSARY

1. To enter, complete an Official Entry Form or 3"× 5" index card by hand-printing, in plain block letters, your complete name, address, phone number and age, and mailing it to: Harlequin Fashion A Whole New You Sweepstakes, P.O. Box 9056, Buffalo, NY 14269-9056.

   No responsibility is assumed for lost, late or misdirected mail. Entries must be sent separately with first class postage affixed, and be received no later than December 31, 1991 for eligibility.

2. Winners will be selected by D.L. Blair, Inc., an independent judging organization whose decisions are final, in random drawings to be held on January 30, 1992 in Blair, NE at 10:00 a.m. from among all eligible entries received.

3. The prizes to be awarded and their approximate retail values are as follows: Grand Prize — A brand-new Mercury Sable LS plus a trip for two (2) to Paris, including round-trip air transportation, six (6) nights hotel accommodation, a $1,400 meal/spending money stipend and $2,000 cash toward a new fashion wardrobe (approximate value: $28,000) or $15,000 cash; two (2) Second Prizes — A trip to Paris, including round-trip air transportation, six (6) nights hotel accommodation, a $1,400 meal/spending money stipend and $2,000 cash toward a new fashion wardrobe (approximate value: $11,000) or $5,000 cash; three (3) Third Prizes — $2,000 cash toward a new fashion wardrobe. All prizes are valued in U.S. currency. Travel award air transportation is from the commercial airport nearest winner's home. Travel is subject to space and accommodation availability, and must be completed by June 30, 1993. Sweepstakes offer is open to residents of the U.S. and Canada who are 21 years of age or older as of December 31, 1991, except residents of Puerto Rico, employees and immediate family members of Torstar Corp., its affiliates, subsidiaries, and all agencies, entities and persons connected with the use, marketing, or conduct of this sweepstakes. All federal, state, provincial, municipal and local laws apply. Offer void wherever prohibited by law. Taxes and/or duties, applicable registration and licensing fees, are the sole responsibility of the winners. Any litigation within the province of Quebec respecting the conduct and awarding of a prize may be submitted to the Régie des loteries et courses du Québec. All prizes will be awarded; winners will be notified by mail. No substitution of prizes is permitted.

4. Potential winners must sign and return any required Affidavit of Eligibility/Release of Liability within 30 days of notification. In the event of noncompliance within this time period, the prize may be awarded to an alternate winner. Any prize or prize notification returned as undeliverable may result in the awarding of that prize to an alternate winner. By acceptance of their prize, winners consent to use of their names, photographs or their likenesses for purposes of advertising, trade and promotion on behalf of Torstar Corp. without further compensation. Canadian winners must correctly answer a time-limited arithmetical question in order to be awarded a prize.

5. For a list of winners (available after 3/31/92), send a separate stamped, self-addressed envelope to: Harlequin Fashion A Whole New You Sweepstakes, P.O. Box 4694, Blair, NE 68009.

PREMIUM OFFER TERMS

To receive your gift, complete the Offer Certificate according to directions. Be certain to enclose the required number of "Fashion A Whole New You" proofs of product purchase (which are found on the last page of every specially marked "Fashion A Whole New You" Harlequin or Silhouette romance novel). Requests must be received no later than December 31, 1991. Limit: four (4) gifts per name, family, group, organization or address. Items depicted are for illustrative purposes only and may not be exactly as shown. Please allow 6 to 8 weeks for receipt of order. Offer good while quantities of gifts last. In the event an ordered gift is no longer available, you will receive a free, previously unpublished Harlequin or Silhouette book for every proof of purchase you have submitted with your request, plus a refund of the postage and handling charge you have included. Offer good in the U.S. and Canada only.

HQFW-SWPR

HARLEQUIN® OFFICIAL SWEEPSTAKES ENTRY FORM

4-FWHRS-2

Complete and return this Entry Form immediately – the more entries you submit, the better your chances of winning!

- Entries must be received by **December 31, 1991.**
- A Random draw will take place on **January 30, 1992.**
- No purchase necessary.

Yes, I want to win a FASHION A WHOLE NEW YOU Classic and Romantic prize from Harlequin:

Name _____ Telephone _____ Age _____

Address _____

City _____ State _____ Zip _____

Return Entries to: **Harlequin FASHION A WHOLE NEW YOU,**
P.O. Box 9056, Buffalo, NY 14269-9056   © 1991 Harlequin Enterprises Limited

PREMIUM OFFER

To receive your free gift, send us the required number of proofs-of-purchase from any specially marked FASHION A WHOLE NEW YOU Harlequin or Silhouette Book with the Offer Certificate properly completed, plus a check or money order (do not send cash) to cover postage and handling payable to Harlequin FASHION A WHOLE NEW YOU Offer. We will send you the specified gift.

OFFER CERTIFICATE

Item	A. ROMANTIC COLLECTOR'S DOLL (Suggested Retail Price $60.00)	B. CLASSIC PICTURE FRAME (Suggested Retail Price $25.00)
# of proofs-of-purchase	18	12
Postage and Handling	$3.50	$2.95
Check one	☐	☐

Name _____

Address _____

City _____ State _____ Zip _____

Mail this certificate, designated number of proofs-of-purchase and check or money order for postage and handling to: Harlequin FASHION A WHOLE NEW YOU Gift Offer, P.O. Box 9057, Buffalo, NY 14269-9057. Requests must be received by December 31, 1991.

ONE PROOF-OF-PURCHASE

4-FWHRP-2

To collect your fabulous free gift you must include the necessary number of proofs-of-purchase with a properly completed Offer Certificate.

© 1991 Harlequin Enterprises Limited

See previous page for details.